He shouldn't stand here watching her.

Ryan knew he should move, prepare for bed, do anything other than get taken in by the implied intimacy of Kit's small gestures—her stepping out of her shoes, taking the pins from her hair.

He didn't move.

Kit held the corsage she'd worn at the wedding and lifted it to her face and breathed in. Just at that moment, she raised her lashes, and their gazes met and locked. All day he'd been touching her, caressing and even kissing her, to get even for being placed in such a ridiculous position. Now he wanted to do all those things for a different reason.

How was he supposed to spend all night with her?

Judith Janeway began her career as a published author at age ten when she won an essay contest run by her local newspaper. She enjoys a challenging career as a writer, researcher and lecturer in health psychology, but she has never abandoned her lifelong dream of writing romance fiction.

She and her husband live in Northern California with their three children. When asked what she does in her spare time, she usually responds, 'What spare time?'

AN ACCIDENTAL MARRIAGE

BY
JUDITH JANEWAY

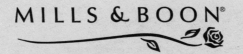

To the memory of my mother, Jane Culbertson, and to
my father, John Culbertson, who in their fifty-seven years
of marriage taught me a lot about true love.

*First published in Great Britain 2000
Harlequin Mills & Boon Limited,
Eton House, 18-24 Paradise Road, Richmond, Surrey TW9 1SR*

© Judith Wrubel 1997

ISBN 0 263 82069 6

*Set in Times Roman 10½ on 12 pt.
02-0004-49552*

*Printed and bound in Spain
by Litografia Rosés, S.A., Barcelona*

Chapter One

Kit Kendrick wiped the condensation from the taxi's window. This was the place, all right. No one could miss that pink-and-white sign—The Happily Ever After Wedding Chapel. She handed her fare plus tip to the driver over the front seat and scrambled out, hauling her overnight bag with her. What in the world had possessed Lindsay to elope to Reno? Whatever madness it was—it had to be stopped.

She sidestepped a mound of plowed snow and hurried up the path to the entrance of the knotty pine A-frame chapel. Organ music floated out into the chill air. Lindsay wouldn't start without her, would she?

The door to the foyer opened before she could reach it. She rushed across the threshold, past the man who held the door open for her. Except for him, the foyer was empty.

"Kit Kendrick?" he asked.

She turned to face him. Tall and dark said it all—dark

hair, dark eyes, dark suit. Even his closely shaven chin
hinted at a dark beard. "Yes?" she said.

"We'd just about given up on you." He reached for
her overnight bag. "Here, I'll take care of this for you."

She let him pull the bag from her fingers. "And you
are…?" she asked.

"Sorry, I thought Lindsay told you. I'm Ryan Holt."
His smile came in a flash of white teeth and one dimple.

He was Lindsay's type, all right, too good-looking for
his own good, and too charming for hers. But he wasn't
the man she'd expected. She looked around the empty
lobby and back to Ryan Holt. "I thought…I understood
that she was going to marry…" She hesitated…how to
put this?

"Jeff Sanderson?" Ryan filled in for her. "She is, or
she will if we don't miss our scheduled time. I'm the best
man."

That explained it. Lindsay had said something last
night about Jeff's friend, but Kit had been too bowled
over by Lindsay's news to pay attention. All she'd
wanted to do was talk Lindsay out of this crazy idea.
"Do you think you can talk some sense into Jeff?"

He frowned at her. "What do you mean?"

"You know, convince him to wait and do this the right
way."

"'The right way'?" he echoed. "You mean with
seven bridesmaids, five hundred guests, an orchestra and
sit-down dinner all guaranteed to bankrupt her father?"

Wasn't that just like a man to think with his bankbook?
"It would take a lot more than that to bankrupt Warren
Franklin, but that's not what I meant. It's going to break
her mother's heart." That really was the crux of the mat-
ter. She couldn't bear the thought of anyone hurting Mary
Franklin.

"Lindsay's not a child," Ryan said. "Isn't she going to be thirty next month?"

Kit's back stiffened. "What do you mean—that she's desperate? Lindsay's been engaged twice and had many more proposals than that. She could have married a long time ago. She was just waiting for the right man."

"There you are, then. Jeff must be the right man. And they're both old enough to know their own minds."

Why was she wasting her time talking to him? He was no help at all. "Where's Lindsay?" she asked.

"In the ladies' room, right down the hall, waiting for you."

"Why didn't you say so?" She turned to head down the hallway.

"Wait a minute, will you?" Ryan called to her.

She turned. "What?" She couldn't keep the irritation out of her voice. He should be helping her stop them.

"You'll need these." He'd put her bag down somewhere and now approached her holding a large white florist's box.

She took the box. "What's this?"

"The usual—bride's bouquet, maid of honor's corsage. I've already taken out the boutonnieres. I'll take Jeff's to him while you're collecting Lindsay."

"Where is Jeff, anyway?"

"In the men's room trying not to hyperventilate."

"What? Look, if he's having second thoughts, then we'd really be doing them a favor to intervene right now."

"His only fear is that Lindsay will change her mind. And Lindsay has gone on record saying she wouldn't marry him until you got here." He glanced down at his watch. "We're scheduled for ten minutes from now. So, please, go get Lindsay."

Even though he said "please," he delivered it as an order. Maybe he was used to people jumping to attention and carrying out his commands. If so, today was going to be a new experience for him.

She turned away without replying and headed for the door marked Brides. She'd get Lindsay, all right. She'd get her and get them both out of here herself, since Ryan Holt was going to be such an obstructionist.

She pushed open the swinging door to the ladies' room and found Lindsay standing in front of a full-length mirror. Lindsay spun around, and the full skirt of her pink wool dress whirled around her legs.

"Kit, you're here at last." Lindsay ran to her, grabbed her by the arm and dragged her into the middle of the room. "I've been waiting and waiting for you. What's in the box?"

"Flowers." Kit glanced around for somewhere to put them down. A low counter with a mirror lined one wall, and a sofa stood against another. "Look, Lindsay, we have to talk."

Lindsay took the box from her, carried it to the sofa and pulled off the lid. "White roses *and* white orchids— aren't they beautiful?" She lifted the ribbon-festooned bouquet from its tissue paper nest, and the scent of roses and something else more exotic filled the room. "Ryan brought these, didn't he? He's so sweet. He's helped us arrange everything. Jeff is so lucky to have a friend like Ryan."

"*Sweet* is one adjective I wouldn't have used to describe Ryan Holt," Kit said.

Lindsay gently returned the bouquet to the box. "I know. He's really gorgeous, isn't he? Not as gorgeous as Jeff, of course, but quite yummy in his own way."

She'd pass on discussing Ryan. She and Lindsay had

never been attracted to the same type of man. Besides, she had something more important to talk about. How was she going to convince Lindsay to give up this impulsive plan of hers?

"What's this?" Lindsay pulled the tissue away from the corsage which nestled in one corner of the box.

"That's supposed to be for me," Kit said. "But put it down, Lindsay, and let's talk. This isn't right, and you know it."

"Of course not. Only my grandmother wears corsages."

Kit tossed her purse onto the sofa. How like Lindsay to deliberately misunderstand her. "I'm talking about the wedding."

Lindsay stared down at the corsage in her hand for a few seconds, her brow wrinkled in a small frown.

"Lindsay?" Kit prompted.

Lindsay looked up at her with a brilliant smile. "I've got it. We'll put it in your hair." She carried the flowers to the low counter and opened her makeup kit. "Come over here and I'll do it for you." When Kit didn't move, she glanced over at her and said, "Why don't you take off that heavy coat? You must be roasting." She went back to pulling things out of her bag.

Kit shrugged out of her coat and tossed it onto her purse. "Don't get married today."

Lindsay stopped in midmotion and turned slowly to face Kit. "But I love him," she said, as if that explained everything.

"You've known him only four weeks. You can't know him well enough to marry him."

"*You* work with him. Is he different at work? Is there something I should know?"

"No, of course not. He's a great guy or I wouldn't

have introduced you to him in the first place. But think about your parents. What about your mother?''

''That's just it. I am thinking about her. You know she's not supposed to have any stress. What would planning a big wedding do to her?''

''And what's it going to do to her when you tell her you've just run off and married someone you've known only one month?''

''That's just it. I won't do that. I'll let them meet Jeff and give them time to get to know him. Then I'll tell them.'' She came around behind Kit, put her hands on her shoulders and steered her toward a wooden chair in front of the mirror. ''Now, sit down so I can fix your hair.''

Kit sank into the chair and stared at Lindsay's reflection in the mirror. Why couldn't she think of an argument that would sway her?

Lindsay undid the clip that restrained Kit's hair and busied herself with brush and hairpins. ''You have such beautiful auburn hair.''

''It's red,'' she replied almost automatically. Those were the first words they'd ever said to each other—Kit, a scholarship student at the exclusive Elizabeth Woods School for Girls, and Lindsay, one of the elite crowd who'd been enrolled at birth.

''Is it naturally curly?'' Lindsay continued.

''Naturally frizzy,'' Kit said, and smiled. They'd reminded each other of their first encounter many times over the years.

''I wish I had hair like yours,'' Lindsay declared, just as she had years ago. How Lindsay, whose blond hair hung like a perfect shiny silk curtain down to her shoulders, could claim to envy Kit's unmanageable mop, was a mystery Kit had never understood. But, even though she hadn't believed her then, and didn't believe her now, she loved her for saying it.

"Now, hold still." Lindsay pinned up Kit's hair and secured the flowers into place at the back of Kit's head. "It's sort of a Gibson Girl effect. Very pretty."

There was a knock at the door. "Lindsay?" Ryan called through the door. "Are you ready? We're running a little late."

"Just give us one more minute," Lindsay called back.

Kit stood up and faced her friend. "We're probably closer than most sisters, and I want you to be happy. But I love your Mom, too. I know you think Mary would do anything you asked, but she didn't have to take me in when my Mom died. She didn't have to love me and take care of me, but she did because she's a wonderful person. I can't bear to think of how this will hurt her. Please don't get married today. Wait just a few more months. What difference can a few months make?"

"Why do you keep trying to change my mind? It's what I want. It's what Jeff wants. It's going to be forever, but I want forever to start today. Please, Kit, wish me happiness. Be my maid of honor the way you always promised you would when we were kids."

She had to face it. Lindsay was going to get married, and nothing she could say would stop her. Mary and Warren would be hurt, no question. If only there was some way to protect them. She'd tried her best, but beneath all of Lindsay's blond, blue-eyed softness lay a will of iron.

There was another knock on the door. "All right, already," Kit called. "We're coming."

Lindsay brightened and grabbed Kit in a fierce hug. "You'll never know how much this means to me. I'm so happy."

Kit returned the embrace. "I'm happy for you." It was almost true. Just the slight sting of tears behind her eyelids belied her words.

Ryan leaned against the wall and watched Jeff pace the corridor. In all the years he'd known Jeff, he'd never seen him so worked up. That redheaded friend of Lindsay's had better not throw a monkey wrench into this wedding. Jeff would probably really fall apart if she did.

Jeff paused in his pacing and turned to Ryan. "I can't tell you how much I appreciate your taking care of all the arrangements."

"You already have—about five times." He couldn't help grinning. Poor Jeff. Is this what love did to you?

Jeff gave him a lopsided smile. "I guess I have, but it bears repeating. I'll never forget this. I mean it. If I can ever return the favor, just let me know."

Ryan shook his head. "Since I don't plan on getting married, I don't think I'll be taking you up on that."

"You say that now, but wait until you meet the right woman."

There wasn't any point in arguing with him. Ryan had been through this with too many other people. They all said the same thing. Some of them were still married, and some weren't. But marriage had changed every one of them, which was fine if that was what they wanted. He couldn't see it for himself.

The door to the ladies' room opened and Lindsay came floating out with Kit right behind, still not looking too happy. Not that her mood mattered as long as she was going to be at the ceremony.

"We're ready," Lindsay announced, tucking her arm through Jeff's and gazing up at him with a thousand-watt smile. Jeff stood there as if he'd been poleaxed, Ryan thought. Understandable. Lindsay was a beauty—tall, blond and very nicely put together. Funny, though, with Kit Kendrick standing next to her, she appeared a little washed out.

Just at that moment, Kit glanced over at him. With her jaw set stubbornly and her brows drawn together, she looked like she was blaming him for something. He pushed away from the wall and strolled over to her.

"What?" she snapped.

"That's what I was going to ask."

"You're the one standing there with your eyebrow raised like a semaphore signal. Only I don't know what you're signaling."

"I was just wondering if everything's all right."

"Everything's great. Couldn't be better. I'm about to watch my best friend get married without her parents present or even knowing what's going on."

"Couples run away to get married all the time. What's the big deal?"

"You clearly wouldn't understand," she said, turning away. The rose-and-orchid corsage lay nestled in the red curls pinned up at the back of her head.

"You wore my flowers, after all," he said. "They look very pretty in your hair like that."

She jerked back to face him, her mouth still pursed in disapproval, but her cheeks pink.

"Lindsay's idea, not mine," she said. "And what do you mean, *your* flowers?"

"I helped Jeff organize everything."

"So you're the one who picked The Happily Ever After Wedding Chapel. Why? Was Drive-Through Weddings closed for the winter?"

"Granted, it's not Grace Cathedral, but they don't

care.'' He gestured with his head to Jeff and Lindsay. ''So why should you?''

She frowned and looked ready to launch into him again. He held up his hands. ''Wait,'' he said, ''don't tell me—I wouldn't understand. Right?''

''Exactly.'' She tipped her chin up and exposed the long line of her throat.

She really had an extraordinarily long neck, or maybe just having her hair up like that made it look longer than it was. And something about the very fair skin that went with red hair invited notions of nibbling and nuzzling. Wait a minute. He'd better not forget the temperament that went with that red hair. She was a scrapper, and right now she had it in for him for some reason.

''What are we waiting for?'' Kit asked. ''A minute ago you were about to put a dent in the ladies' room door to get us out here. Now that we're here, we're standing around.''

''We missed our reserved time. But Mrs. Byrd said she'd perform the ceremony for Jeff and Lindsay next.'' Ryan checked his watch. ''Which would be right about now.''

As if on cue, strains of the wedding march floated down the corridor, followed by a burst of noisy chatter and laughter.

He turned to Jeff and Lindsay, who were so wrapped up in each other they didn't seem to hear the commotion in the foyer. ''It's time,'' he said, loud enough to pierce their dream state.

''It's time?'' Jeff said, blinking at him. ''Are we ready? Do we have everything?''

Poor Jeff. He'd always been a great executive, could manage multiple projects at once. Now look at him. Ryan patted his breast pocket. "I have the ring right here. Just follow Kit and me."

He offered his arm to Kit. "I believe we're supposed to lead the parade."

She stared at his arm a moment and then solemnly placed her hand in the crook of his elbow. She still looked unhappy. No, he was wrong. She looked sad. He reached his free hand over and patted hers where its paleness lay in stark contrast to his dark sleeve.

"I also have extra handkerchiefs if you need one during the ceremony," he said in her ear.

"Don't be silly. Why would I cry? I'm not the one getting married."

Kit stood next to Lindsay and watched the blue-haired Mrs. Byrd bustle from the electric organ to a spot flanked by two white wicker baskets of dusty plastic gladioli. It looked like Mrs. Byrd ran the whole show by herself. Maybe she'd gone to the same school for efficiency experts Ryan Holt had.

If she turned her head slightly to the right, he would be in her line of vision. She'd keep focused on Mrs. Byrd. Something about Ryan made her uneasy. Particularly when he fixed her with that dark gaze and looked like he was about to eat her up.

Mrs. Byrd held a large black book open in front of her, but she didn't consult it. She smiled at Lindsay and Jeff. "Dearly beloved," she began.

In a few minutes, Lindsay would be married. Her best friend, her almost sister, would go off and have her own family. She'd already left her in spirit, if not in fact. When they'd walked out of the ladies' room, Lindsay had gone over to Jeff and acted as if no one else in the world existed. She'd never acted like that around a man before, not even with her two previous fiancés.

It was no big surprise, really. Kit had expected it for years—even planned for it during Lindsay's two previous engagements. Lindsay needed to be married, to belong to someone who was devoted to her.

She'd see a lot less of Lindsay now. That was what had happened with her other married friends. After a while they lost touch. Being married did that to people. And once they had children, they found they just didn't have anything in common with their single friends.

Mrs. Byrd was at her electric organ once again hammering out Mendelssohn. Kit looked around. Was the ceremony over already? How had she missed the whole thing?

Lindsay and Jeff practically skipped out of the room. Ryan offered his arm to her. She lifted her gaze and met his dark eyes. His brows were drawn together in something that looked like concern.

"Maybe you'd be better off crying," he said.

"What do you mean?"

"I don't know. You look so sad."

She tilted her chin. "Don't be silly," she said, and grabbed his arm. "Let's go." It was perfectly ridiculous to be marching out arm in arm as if they were in some formal ceremony instead of insta-vows at a marriage mill, but Ryan seemed to have his own sense of how things were supposed to be.

Lindsay and Jeff were waiting for them in the foyer. "There you are," Lindsay said. "What took you so long? Can you believe it? We're actually married." She reached up and kissed Jeff full on the mouth. Then Jeff kissed her back.

Kit plastered a smile on her face and waited for them

to come up for air. She stole a look at her watch. They'd probably want to go somewhere for a late lunch. If they hurried up, she could catch the evening flight back to San Francisco and not have to stay over in Reno. She'd feel a little less strange once she was back in her own apartment.

Lindsay and Jeff finally pulled apart. "We have to get our coats," Lindsay said, and headed back toward the ladies' room. She turned suddenly and called, "Kit."

Before Kit could open her mouth to say a word, Lindsay sent her bridal bouquet flying through the air. Instinctively, Kit put out her hands and caught it.

"Gotcha," Lindsay said, laughing.

"Tricked me is more like it," Kit replied. Lindsay knew darn well she would never purposely have put herself in the line of fire of a bridal bouquet.

"What's the matter?" Ryan asked. "This should cheer you up. Doesn't catching the bouquet mean you're supposed to be the next one to get married?"

"Don't be silly. That's just a stupid superstition."

"Stop saying that."

"Saying what?"

"That I'm silly. I am *not* silly."

"Fine," she said, pushing the bouquet into his hands. "Then you can have the bouquet, because I don't ever intend to get married."

Kit stared out the window of Ryan's car at the snow-laden pines and the heavy drifts by the side of the highway. Jeff's and Lindsay's voices came to her as a soft murmur from the back seat. Lindsay's bouquet rested in her lap where Ryan had placed it, giving her a look that dared her to refuse it. The flowers' perfume drifted to her, borne on the warm air from the car heater.

"How much farther would you say it is to the cabin?"
Ryan asked.

Kit bit her lip to hide her smile. Boy, was he in for a
surprise. Lindsay's great-grandmother, used to a more ur-
ban setting, had dubbed the family lakefront home a
"cabin," and the name had stuck. It hadn't occurred to
Lindsay that Ryan and Jeff would be expecting a small
rustic cottage.

"We're almost there. I'll give you warning before we
come to the turn," she said. It made sense that Lindsay
would want to spend the first night of her honeymoon
here. Lake Tahoe provided a beautiful setting, and the
family country house was probably more luxurious than
any hotel they could stay in. Lindsay had insisted that
Ryan and Kit come along and have a meal to celebrate
the wedding, and Kit could hardly refuse. She'd just
make sure to leave enough time to make it back to the
airport.

"It's incredible here with the lake and the mountains,"
Ryan said. "I've never seen any place so beautiful."

"You've never been here before?" Kit asked. "I
thought you were from San Francisco."

"I just moved there a couple of weeks ago. I've toured
the city, but I haven't seen the rest of California yet."

"It's the third left from here, between the stone pillars." She turned to Lindsay in the back seat. "You're
sure no one's going to be using the cabin this weekend?"

"I'm sure. Mom and Dad have some big party they're
going to tonight."

All of the houses along this stretch of the lake were
set well back from the road, and were clearly fairly elegant. Ryan had reduced speed and was eyeing each property as they passed. He'd probably guessed the truth by
now. As he turned into the drive that led to the house,

he slowed the car to a crawl and stared around him. Just past a curve in the drive, the two-story house built of river rock and cedar stood among the tall pines.

"Cabin, huh?" he said, and brought the car to a halt in front of the wide front porch.

"That's what Great-Grandma Franklin always called it," Lindsay said. "Look, you two, this is our plan. Ryan and Jeff will go on down the road to the store and get some food. And Kit and I will go in and get the fires lit and make everything nice and cozy. Having a meal here will be much nicer than going to some old restaurant."

Kit got out of the car before Ryan could reply to Lindsay. It wasn't exactly an equal division of labor, since getting the fires lit probably meant simply striking a few matches—the caretaker would have laid the wood and kindling in all the fireplaces already. But she would like a few minutes alone with Lindsay to make sure Lindsay knew that she really was happy for her. Plus, she could use some time away from Ryan. She almost had the feeling that Lindsay and Jeff were pairing them off together.

Lindsay followed Kit up the front steps as Ryan drove off. Lindsay paused and stuck her hand in her purse. "I have the key right here," she said.

But apparently the key was somewhat elusive. Kit stood clutching the bouquet and breathing in the familiar pine-scented air while Lindsay continued to rummage around in her purse.

Suddenly, the door flew open and Mary Franklin stood on the threshold. "Lindsay and Kit! I thought I heard someone drive up. We didn't know you were planning on coming up this weekend." Then her gaze fell on the bridal bouquet in Kit's hands and she fell silent.

Lindsay leaped into the breach. "Mom, you won't believe it. It's the most romantic thing. Kit just got married."

Chapter Two

Kit's mouth fell open. She had to say something, anything—but her very breath stuck in her throat. Mary Franklin gazed at her with eyes at first wide with surprise and then wincing as if in pain. She'd hurt Mary—the very thing she'd dreaded, and it had happened before she could blink. How could Lindsay have done this to her?

Mary recovered before Kit could and hurried toward her, arms wide open. "My dear, how wonderful." She embraced her warmly and kissed her cheek. "Don't stand out here in the cold. Come in and tell me all about it." She ushered them into the wide front hall. "But where is the groom?" she asked, looking over Kit's shoulder.

"He went off with the best man to get some food," Lindsay said. "We thought we'd have a little celebration here."

"And who is the groom? Do I know him?"

"His name is Ryan Holt, and he just swept Kit right off her feet. He's really terrific. Wait until you meet him."

Kit stood like a statue, gripping Lindsay's bridal bouquet in her gloved hands. Lindsay always could talk and look like such a wide-eyed innocent, no matter what she'd been up to that she shouldn't have. This time, though, she'd gone too far.

"I'm...I'm not..." Kit stumbled over the words.

Mary's face creased with concern. "What is it, Kit?"

"She's worried about barging in on you and Dad," Lindsay said quickly. She stood next to Mary and shook her head in warning to Kit. "You told me you had some party or other you had to go to tonight, Mom."

"It was canceled at the last minute, thank heavens. I wouldn't have missed this occasion for the world. Why don't you take off your coats and come into the living room? I want to hear all about it."

Lindsay grabbed Kit by the arm and pulled her toward the stairs. "You know what, Mom? Kit and I would like to leave our things upstairs. Give us a minute to comb our hair. We'll be right down."

Kit tugged her arm free of Lindsay's grip, but followed her up the stairs. She had a thing or two to say to Lindsay. She paused halfway up the staircase and looked back down at Mary, who still stood in the hall gazing at them with a troubled expression. "Where's Warren?" Kit asked her.

"He's down at the dock, of course, checking the lake level," Mary answered, with a smile that almost cleared the worry from her face.

They must have just arrived. Warren always checked the lake first thing when they came up to Tahoe. If Kit hadn't been late meeting Lindsay at the chapel, they'd have been here before Mary and Warren. And Lindsay wouldn't have been able to tell such a lie to her mother.

Kit moved quickly and caught up with Lindsay. Without saying anything, they went straight into Lindsay's room. Lindsay closed the door carefully and leaned her back against it. Kit went straight to the bed and dumped the bouquet, gloves and coat onto it.

"I can't believe you did that," Kit said, her voice barely steady.

"I know you're angry." Lindsay pushed away from the door and slipped out of her own coat and gloves.

"Angry? I'm not angry. I'm furious, shocked, upset and disgusted. Why would you do such a thing? She's going to find out it's not true in about ten minutes, and you're going to look like an idiot."

"She's not going to find out if you and Ryan don't tell her."

"Exactly. Ryan will think you've lost your marbles and will tell Mary and Warren the truth before he dials 911 for the men in white coats to come get you. And what about Jeff? Didn't you just vow 'till death do you part'? Did he sign a prenuptial agreement that amended that to 'or until it's inconvenient for Lindsay'?"

"Jeff will understand," Lindsay said, her face serious. "I didn't want to tell you, but…" Lindsay let the rest of the sentence hang in the air.

"But what?" Kit demanded.

"Mom's heart condition is worse."

"Worse?" Kit could barely breathe the word out. She sank down on the side of the bed.

"Yes, and that's why I didn't want to tell her that I'd gotten married. She's not supposed to have any shocks or stress."

"I didn't know. We had lunch last week and she didn't say a word about it."

"Well, she wouldn't. She's never wanted to talk about it. You know that. We always have to pretend that everything's just fine. She was shocked enough when we told her you'd just gotten married. Think how shocked she'd be if we'd said that *I'd* gotten married.''

'''We' didn't tell her. You did. You could have just as easily said we'd simply been to someone else's wedding.''

"Well, I couldn't think that fast. So this is our story and we have to stick with it. Look, it's just for the afternoon. We'll have a meal with Mom and Dad, then Ryan will drive us to the Reno airport.''

Kit put her fingers to her temples. "It's *not* just for one afternoon as far as Mary and Warren are concerned.''

Lindsay wrinkled her nose. "Quit inviting problems. All you have to do is call them tomorrow and tell them you and Ryan agree it was a mistake to get married.''

"What about Jeff and Ryan? They'll never agree.''

"I'll take care of Jeff. You handle Ryan.''

"Me? He's a complete stranger. What am I supposed to say? Excuse me. You don't know me, but would you mind pretending we're newlyweds? Can't Jeff talk to him?''

"No, there won't be enough time. We have to intercept them before they get to the front door." Lindsay tugged her wedding ring off her finger. "Here, put this on." She grabbed Kit's left hand and attempted to push the ring onto her finger.

"Hey, stop. It doesn't fit." Kit tried to pull her hand away, but Lindsay hung on.

"It has to fit," Lindsay said, her lips pressed tight in determination. "Mom will never believe us if you're not wearing a ring.''

Lindsay was right. Mary wouldn't believe them. And if she guessed the truth, she'd not only have the shock of Lindsay's elopement, she'd suffer the pain of being left out of her daughter's wedding.

"Here, let me," Kit said. She forced the ring past her knuckle. It was way too small. Getting it off wasn't going to be easy. She looked down at the intricately patterned band. It wasn't her size or her taste, but it represented Lindsay's and Jeff's pledge to each other. "How can you bear to part with it?"

"Because I have to. Besides, it's only for the afternoon." She moved toward the door. "Let's go downstairs so we can catch Ryan and Jeff when they drive up. Remember, all you have to do is look deliriously happy, and everyone will believe you just got married."

"I think I can manage the delirious part." What had she gotten herself into?

Ryan turned the car into the drive between the stone pillars and slowly approached the house. "Some cabin Lindsay's family owns," he said to Jeff.

Jeff leaned forward in his seat and looked out the front windshield. "It's huge, isn't it. It was built as a summer home around the turn of the century. All part of being one of *the* San Francisco Franklins. I'm glad Lindsay wants to wait a bit before I'm introduced as her husband. I'm not sure I'm ready to face them."

"You think they're snobs?"

"Lindsay's certainly not, so I'd say no. But they're still an old family with old money and an only child—except for Kit, of course."

He slowed the car as he approached the house. Kit and Lindsay emerged from the front doorway. "What do you mean, except for Kit? She's not related, is she?"

"Not by blood. But the family took her in as a foster child when her mother died. She and Lindsay think of each other as sisters. She caught your interest, didn't she?''

He didn't have time to answer. Kit and Lindsay dashed down the front steps and into the path of the car. Ryan jammed on the brakes and the car came to a jolting halt. ''What the hell?'' He switched off the engine and jerked the keys out of the ignition.

Kit ran up and pulled his door open. He jumped out and grabbed her by the shoulders. ''What kind of crazy trick was that?'' he demanded. ''Don't you know the roads are icy? I could have skidded and run you over.''

She slipped her arms around his neck, closed her eyes and kissed him smack on the mouth. He staggered a little under the force of her attack. What the...? His hands slid down her back and came to rest on her hips. He tightened his grip to push her away, but the softness of her mouth pressed against his momentarily paralyzed him. Suddenly she opened her eyes. How could he not have noticed her eyes were green?

''I'm sorry,'' she whispered against his mouth.

Her words mobilized him, and he pushed her a few inches away.

''All right, you lovebirds,'' Lindsay called. ''Break it up, and help us carry in these groceries.''

Ryan jerked his head around. Lindsay and Jeff stood on the other side of the car, each holding a loaded grocery bag. Jeff winked at him and jerked his head ever so slightly toward the porch. He shifted his gaze to the front of the house and to the couple who stood there—the man tall and silver-haired, the woman an older version of Lindsay. They waved and smiled. He nodded, smiled back and, like a grinning ventriloquist, said to Kit, ''What the hell is going on?''

''They're Lindsay's parents. She told them we got

married today, because she doesn't want them to know about Jeff yet. So, please, play along just for this afternoon.''

He gazed straight into her eyes. "It's a joke, right? Jeff put you up to this."

"No joke," she said, and slid her hands down his chest. "I hate it myself. But Lindsay's mom has a heart condition, and the shock might be too much for her."

"It's a very bad idea."

Kit turned her gaze to the scene on the porch, and Ryan looked, too. Jeff now had both bags of groceries, and Lindsay, one hand on each parent's arm, was trying to convince them to go back inside the house. "We'll be right there," Kit called. The Franklins waved to them once more and let themselves be ushered through the doorway. She faced him again. "Please. You have to help me."

"No. Lies like that always come back to haunt you. We'll just go tell them the truth, and let Jeff and Lindsay sort it out."

He started off toward the house. Kit stayed at his side all the way to the front steps. Suddenly, with a smothered cry, she fell. He turned toward her. She sat on the ground, one leg in front of her, the other bent under her full skirt, which spread around her on the icy pavement.

"Are you okay?" he asked, reaching down to help her up.

She batted his hand away. "I'm fine."

He stood back and waited while she pushed herself upright. The second she put her full weight on her foot her face contorted in pain and she crumpled. Ryan caught her before she fell all the way to the ground.

He held her up, one arm around her waist. "You must have sprained your ankle."

"I'm perfectly fine," she said, grabbing the front of his coat for balance.

"Yeah, right." He swung her up into his arms.

She clutched at his neck, her hands icy.

"You're freezing, too." He carried her up the steps to the front door. She shivered a little and nestled her forehead against his neck.

Jeff opened the door as soon as they approached, as if he'd been watching from inside, waiting for them. Lindsay stood next to him.

"How romantic," Lindsay said with a sigh. "You're carrying her over the threshold."

"Kit slipped on the ice," he explained. "I think she…"

Before he could finish, Kit scissor-kicked her legs and slipped out of his arms. She landed solidly on both feet without flinching.

He stared at her. "Your ankle…" he began.

She wound her arms around his neck and smiled up at him. "I told you I was perfectly all right." Her tone was light, but her gaze was serious.

He reached up and pulled her hands from his neck. "You tricked me."

"*Please* play along," she pleaded under her breath. "It's very important." She turned and faced the Franklins, who were standing nearby, smiling uncertainly at him. "This is Ryan Holt," she announced to them. "Ryan, I'd like you to meet Mary and Warren Franklin."

They stepped forward to greet him, their smiles warm and welcoming now. He couldn't refuse to shake their hands, but Kit Kendrick wouldn't get away with manipulating him.

"Mrs. Franklin," he said, "pleasure to meet you." Her hand felt as fragile as a porcelain teacup in his. He barely squeezed it. Ryan turned to the older man. "Mr. Franklin, how do you do?" This time he got a firm handshake plus a friendly pat on his arm.

"Call me Warren, please. No need to stand on ceremony with family, you know."

This was his cue. He had to cut through this tangle. He glanced at Jeff, but Jeff avoided looking at him. He turned his gaze to Kit. "We're not really married. Are we, Kit?"

A hush fell over the group. Kit hugged his arm and tilted her head against his shoulder. "I can't believe it, either. It all seems so unreal."

Lindsay and Jeff both laughed. He'd have something to say to Jeff later. But right now, he was going to deal with Kit.

Mary Franklin moved toward the wide doorway to the adjoining room. "I must say you both look dazed," she said. "But it will all seem real soon enough. Why are we standing in the hall? Come into the living room."

She led the way into a vast room with a beamed ceiling and massive stone fireplace at one end. Ryan snagged Kit by the wrist and kept her from joining the others.

"I'm sorry, Ryan," she whispered to him. "Really, I am. But can't you please just play along for a couple of hours?"

He bent his head toward her. "I will not be manipulated."

"It wasn't my idea. Lindsay set it up. Do you think *I* like the idea of pretending to be married to *you?*" Even whispered, the words carried a feeling of vehemence.

He opened his mouth to reply and quickly snapped it shut. She made marriage to him sound positively repulsive. Is that what she thought of him? "So let's stop this

right now.'' He broke away from her and strode toward
the end of the room where the others were already seated.

"Ryan,'' Kit called to him, but he ignored her. As he
approached, Mary Franklin looked up, her eyes wide.

"Is everything all right?'' she asked.

"No, it isn't,'' he said.

"What…'' Mary began to rise from her chair, but halfway up she put her hand to her head and sank back onto
the cushions.

"Mom?'' Lindsay leaned forward in her chair.

"Mary, what is it?'' Warren stood up to cross to her.

"Mary!'' Kit cried out, and raced across the room to
kneel at her side. "Are you all right?'' She took Mary's
hands in hers and gazed at her face.

Mary blinked rapidly and gave a little laugh. "I'm fine.
I just stood up too fast, that's all. You know what that's
like.''

Warren seemed to take her at her word and returned
to his seat, but Kit remained kneeling at her side. "Are
you sure?'' Kit asked.

"Of course I'm sure.'' Mary patted Kit's cheek, her
hand stark white even against Kit's fair skin.

What if Kit was right, and Mary Franklin would become ill if she suffered a shock? Ryan shifted his feet
and stuffed his hands in his pockets. Now what was he
going to do?

"I want to hear what Ryan has to say,'' Mary said.

Kit turned her head toward him, her gaze silently accusing him.

"Mrs. Franklin,'' he began.

"Please, call me Mary. As Warren said, you're family
now.''

"Mary, then,'' he said with a smile. "I feel as if we're
imposing on you and Warren. We thought we'd have

something to eat and get back to San Francisco, but I don't want to interfere with your plans for the day.''

''We couldn't possibly have any other plans except to celebrate your marriage. This is a wonderful, happy occasion. I confess that it's also a tremendous surprise, but a very nice one. Sit down, please.'' She gestured to a nearby love seat.

He sat down. Mary shooed Kit over to sit next to him. She slid onto the love seat, her thigh brushing his in the crowded space. She leaned toward him and breathed, ''Thanks,'' into his ear, then straightened again. He caught the scent of roses as she moved her head and he turned to gaze at her profile. She had such a lovely neck. So lovely that he hadn't noticed her very stubborn chin.

Maybe he should show her that she hadn't cornered the market on stubbornness. He may have given in to her ploy to get him to act like a bridegroom, but he didn't have to make it easy for her. She was the one who walked up to him and kissed him without any forewarning. Maybe he'd see how she liked being blindsided.

He put his arm casually around her shoulders. She turned and favored him with a radiant smile, the little liar. He pulled her against his side. Her smile faltered and she resisted slightly, but he increased the pressure until she let her weight sink against him.

Warren cleared his throat. ''Jeff here told us he's responsible for bringing you two together.''

''Yes, you might say my old friend Jeff is responsible for the whole thing.'' Ryan glanced at Jeff sitting by himself in an easy chair. Jeff gave him his most innocent grin. Wait until he got him alone.

''It sounds like a whirlwind romance,'' Mary said. It was an opening, a question.

''You could say that it was absolutely instantaneous,

right, darling?'' He bent his head and nuzzled Kit's neck. She went completely rigid but didn't pull away. He could feel her pulse pounding where his lips touched the silky skin of her neck.

He pulled back and gazed at her. She wouldn't meet his gaze, but a red flush spread from her neck up to her cheeks. Score one for his side.

''And your parents?'' Mary asked.

''His parents are dead,'' Kit said quickly. ''Car crash five years ago.''

''I'm sorry to hear that,'' Mary said.

His parents would be sorry to hear it themselves, since they were both under the impression they were still alive and kicking.

''And he has no other family,'' Kit added.

He turned his gaze on her. What a little devil she was. A red-haired, green-eyed mass murderer.

She gazed back at him with wide innocent eyes and gave him another dose of her luminous, only-for-you smile.

''Well, Ryan,'' Warren said, ''you have a family now, because when you married Kit you got us as part of the package.''

''Thank you,'' he replied, his voice unaccountably husky. They were really nice people. It was pretty mean to trick them like this. ''Kit and I think families are pretty important. So important that we're going to start working on one of our own very soon, aren't we, sweetheart?'' And without giving her a chance to reply he bent his head and kissed her on the mouth.

She went completely still, her shoulder muscles rigid beneath his hand. If his mouth wasn't otherwise engaged, he'd have laughed out loud. Score two for his side.

He'd meant to kiss her quickly, but her lips, at first

tight and firm, softened, yielded to his and, without using any force at all, held him prisoner. He couldn't move. Wait a minute. He could move. He put his free arm around her and pulled her closer.

"I think it's time to break out the champagne." Lindsay's voice broke through the fog that had begun to creep into his brain.

He pulled away and stared at Kit. How had she done that? She'd had the same effect on him when she'd kissed him outside. He glanced around at the others. Warren and Mary were beaming and didn't seem to have noticed anything unusual.

Jeff winked at him and grinned.

Lindsay was on her feet and heading out of the room. "Want to help me with the bubbly, Jeff?" she asked over her shoulder.

"Sure thing." Jeff was on his feet and out of the room in an instant.

Ryan returned his gaze to Kit. She was pink to her hairline, and her smile looked a little strained.

Mary leaned forward in her chair. "I'm so delighted you came here to celebrate. Warren and I will not hear of you going back to San Francisco. You *must* stay here tonight. I insist. Warren and I will go back, and we'll take Lindsay and your friend Jeff with us."

Great. That was all he needed, to be stuck here overnight as half of a supposed honeymoon couple. The whole deception had gone way too far already. "You're very kind," he said. "But Kit and I have already made plans for tonight, haven't we, darling?" As the new "husband," he must have some rights—like where he'd spend his wedding night. And this groom was going to spend his alone in his own apartment.

*   *   *

Kit pulled slightly away from Ryan. She'd had about all she could take of this lovey-dovey stuff. He tightened his hold on her shoulder for a second before relaxing his grip and letting her put a fraction of an inch between them.

Why had he kissed her? She understood his urge to get even, but the declaration of intent to produce children right away made him more than even. He hadn't needed to kiss her, too.

She slanted a look at him. He must have caught some movement out of the corner of his eye, because he turned his head, his eyebrow already arched in inquiry.

"Everything all right?" he asked with a little tilt of his mouth that told her he knew darn well everything was not all right, and that he wasn't helping matters much.

She set her jaw. "Everything's wonderful," she said between her teeth, while keeping her smile firmly in place. She'd probably have to have her smile surgically removed when she finally managed to get back to San Francisco.

"Jeff tells me you're originally from Chicago," Warren said to Ryan.

"That's right. Jeff and I both worked for the same company in Chicago before he moved out here to work at Calvert Container Corporation. He met Kit at Calvert, introduced us, and the rest, as they say, is history."

Mary leaned forward in her chair. "Does this mean you're moving to Chicago, Kit?"

"No," Kit said quickly. Mary hated the idea of her moving away, and pretend marriage or not, she wasn't going to worry her on that score.

"In fact, I've already moved to San Francisco," Ryan said. "And I start my new job at Calvert on Monday."

"What?" Kit asked, stunned.

"Yes. Isn't it great? I got the job. I was saving the news as a surprise for you later." He raised a hand to stroke her cheek. She nearly knocked it away.

"That's wonderful," Mary said.

Kit stared at Ryan. "Unbelievable."

"Aren't you happy, sweetheart?" Ryan asked. "Now we'll be able to see each other day and night."

Happy? How could she be happy? She'd been counting on never having to see him again when this interminable day finally ended.

"You look pretty surprised, Kit," Warren said. "Apparently, he knows how to keep a secret. Are you mad because he didn't tell you before this?"

Was she mad? She was hopping mad—at Ryan, at Lindsay, and, face it, at herself for letting herself get dragged into this mess. But she couldn't show it—not now.

"I am mad at you, darling," she said with as much syrup as she could stand to put into her words. "Married people shouldn't keep things from each other. You should have told me."

"Sorry, sweetheart," he said, matching her tone, "I won't do it again."

He leaned toward her. He'd better not try that kissing business again. She'd been tormented enough for one day. "It's getting pretty late," she said brightly, and stood up from the love seat. "Why don't I go start fixing something for us to eat? We don't want to be setting out too late."

"Guess what?" Lindsay said from the doorway. "While we've been sitting around, it's blown up a storm."

"That's right." Jeff came around from behind her,

bearing a tray laden with glasses and an open bottle of champagne. "We heard it on the radio in the kitchen. The pass is closed. No one's going anywhere until morning."

Chapter Three

Ryan pushed the bedroom door shut with a firm snap. The sound of running water came through the closed bathroom door. Kit had managed to get first dibs on the bathroom while he'd gone to get his suitcase from the car. Just like a woman. He let his case fall to the floor. It made only a small thump on the thick, padded carpet. Nice carpet. Nice room, too. Just like the rest of the house—luxurious, but homey. Under any other circumstances, he'd really enjoy staying here. Right now, he'd almost prefer to sleep in his car, even if it was below freezing.

Kit's suitcase lay open on the bed, something green and silky peeking from one corner. Was she going to sleep in that? Not that it made any difference to him. He didn't have any romantic interest in her—not after the way she'd tricked him. He eyed the bed more closely. It was pretty small. With all the rooms in this place, they could at least have given them one with a decent-sized bed.

Kit emerged from the bathroom still fully dressed. "Get your suitcase all right?" she asked.

He didn't say anything, just looked down at his case and back at her.

"So what's this," she asked, tilting her chin in that way she had, "the silent treatment?"

He folded his arms across his chest. "We're alone now. There's no point in making idle chitchat."

She dropped her gaze. "I was simply trying to be polite."

"Funny thing, but somehow I'm not in the mood for polite conversation. I just want to get some sleep and get out of here as early as possible tomorrow."

"Do you think that *I* don't? Believe me, tomorrow can't come soon enough." She marched to the foot of the bed and bent over her open suitcase.

He watched her for a moment as she shifted her clothes around in her case, folding and refolding several items.

"Why did Mary give us a room with a single bed?" he asked.

"It's a regular full-size," she replied, without looking up from her suitcase. "You're probably used to a king or queen, so it looks smaller to you. But actually, I thought, under the circumstances, you know…" She slowly straightened and lifted her gaze to meet his.

"You thought what?" he asked. She'd better not ask him to give up the bed. She was probably in the habit of using those green eyes to good effect, but they wouldn't work on him. No, sir.

"I thought you wouldn't mind sleeping on the floor," she replied, slanting her gaze away from him, then back again.

"I'd mind very much. In case you hadn't noticed, it's

snowing outside. Even in here, it would be too cold to spend the whole night on the floor.''

"There are usually extra blankets in the closet.''

"All right, if sharing this bed with me is too much of an affront to your sensibilities, we'll take out the blankets and *you* can sleep on the floor.''

"Me?'' She gave him her big-eyed look of surprise. Not that he was taken in by it.

"Yes, you. You're the one who got me into this farce in the first place.''

"No, I didn't. Lindsay did.''

"I beg to differ with you, but I distinctly remember telling Mary and Warren that we were *not* married, and you contradicted me.''

"I had to do it. I thought you understood.''

"Well, I don't. All I know is that I am stuck here, forced into pretending to spend my wedding night with someone I met less than twelve hours ago. For that I think I deserve the bed.''

Just to make sure she got his point, he crossed to the bed and lay down in the middle, stretching a bit for effect. "It sags a little, but it'll do for one night.'' He put his hands behind his head and shifted his shoulders into a more comfortable position on the pillows. "Aaah,'' he murmured, exhaling noisily.

"Fine,'' she said, her mouth set in a thin line. She strode over to the closet. With one heave of her arm the louvered doors folded aside with a crash. Then silence. "Oh,'' she said in a small voice.

Ryan lifted his head a little to get a better look. The interior of the closet was bare except for a stack of board games on the overhead shelf.

Kit swung away from the closet and approached the bed. "There aren't any blankets,'' she announced.

"So I see," he said, letting his head sink back again.

Kit bent over the bed and lifted a corner of the bed-spread.

"Don't tell me you're getting into bed with all your clothes on."

"Don't be silly. I'm looking to see if there are enough blankets on the bed to divide up."

He sat up and swung his legs over the side of the bed. "How many times do I have to tell you that I'm not silly? If anyone's silly, it's you. Why can't we both sleep in the bed?"

"Because it's not big enough for both of us, for one thing." She flipped the spread back into place.

"And what's the other thing?"

She smoothed the bedspread and didn't reply.

"Go on, tell me. What's the other thing?"

She straightened and fiddled with the wedding band on her third finger. "You, if you want to know."

"Me? What is it? Am I so repulsive you can't bear to be near me even with the lights out and your eyes closed?"

"Don't be…" she started to say.

"If you call me silly one more time, I won't be responsible for my actions."

"There you go. That's just what I meant. You're intimidating."

He rose to his feet. "What on earth are you talking about?"

"All afternoon and evening, you've been—you know—touching me." She tugged at the wedding ring. "Intimidating me."

"Intimidating you? I don't think that's possible. Now, if you want to talk about intimidation, how about me driving along, minding my own business, and you throwing yourself in front of my car and scaring me half to death. Then, I get out, my knees shaking, and you grab me, kiss me and tell me I have to pretend we're married. Now, *that's* intimidation.''

''I couldn't think of any other way of making it look convincing.''

''Right. And I guess you also had to kill off my entire family, too, just to make it look 'convincing,''' he said.

''What?''

''You told Mary and Warren that I was an only child and both my parents were dead.''

''Your parents aren't dead, I suppose?''

''And neither are my five brothers and sisters,'' he added, just to rub it in.

''You have five brothers and sisters?'' she nearly whispered.

''Until today. But then, I was a single man until today.''

''I guess you're really angry at me for making you pretend to be married.''

He wasn't going to deny it, so he said nothing. But even as he stood there, he could feel his irritation draining away. How had she done that? He was mad about it—in his mind he was, anyway—but he couldn't feel quite so mad.

''I don't blame you.'' She went back to worrying the wedding ring. ''I'm as sorry as I can be, but you have to believe me—I never would have done it myself. Lindsay sometimes acts impulsively, and others have to deal with it.''

''I see,'' he said, but all he actually saw was that his righteous indignation had faded and gone. It was damn irritating that she'd talked him out of it, too. Next, she'd convince him to let her have the bed all to herself.

Her third finger was now red from her continual twisting of the ring. For some reason, that irritated him, too.
"What are you doing with that ring?"

She looked down at her hand as if she'd just noticed
that she'd been fiddling with it. "It's too tight. I'm trying
to get it off." She tugged harder.

"Why? You'll have to wear it tomorrow until we
leave."

"I know. I'd just feel better if I could get it off. What
if it's stuck on my finger?" She held up her hand, fingers
splayed, and examined the ring close up.

"It will come off easily in the morning if you'll leave
it alone now. In fact, why don't we both just concentrate
on getting some sleep?"

She dropped her hands to her sides. "That's probably
the best thing." She stepped out of her shoes, bent down
and picked them up. "If you'll divvy up the blankets,
you can have the bed. I'm probably a lot more used to
sleeping on the floor than you are. Lindsay and I always
slept on the floor whenever there were too many guests."

Ryan shoved his hands into his pockets. Great, just
great. At least she could have had the decency to sound
like a martyr. He could have withstood that ploy. All she
had to do was act put upon, and he'd really have enjoyed
taking the bed and letting her sleep on the floor.

He watched as Kit padded over to the straight-backed
wooden chair by the window and put her shoes down
next to it. Okay, she had her shoes off, what would come
off next? She crossed to the bed, got her bag and carried
it to the chair, too. He couldn't stop looking at her feet.

"If you want to use the bathroom—" she broke off.

He lifted his gaze to her face. What had she been saying?

"Why are you staring at my feet?"

"I wasn't staring." He had been, of course. What was it about her walking around fully dressed in her stocking feet? Somehow it made his mind slip into another gear, and not the one he was supposed to be in with this woman. "I was simply staring into space. I'm tired, that's all."

"Me, too. If you want to use the bathroom, go ahead."

That sounded like a very good idea. He should just get ready for bed and go to sleep. It would all be over tomorrow.

Kit lifted her arms and worked at the pins holding the flowers in her hair. She tilted her head slightly forward, her neck bent in a graceful arc, the nape of her neck temptingly exposed.

She pulled the flowers free, and her hair came loose at the same time, falling over her neck in a mass of red curls. He shouldn't stand here watching her. He should act, prepare for bed, do anything other than get taken in by the implied intimacy of her small gestures—her stepping out of her shoes, taking the pins from her hair.

He didn't move.

She held the corsage and looked at it for a moment, then lifted it to her face and breathed in. Just at that moment, she raised her lashes, and their gazes met and locked. All day he'd been touching her, caressing, nuzzling and even kissing her to get even for being placed in such a ridiculous position. Now he wanted to do all those things again, but for a different reason.

Kit lowered the flowers. "I wish you wouldn't do that."

She couldn't read his mind, could she? "Do what?"

"Stare at me—or in my direction. I know you're tired, but from my side it feels like you're staring at me."

"Sorry." He turned away. It probably was just fatigue

that was making him react to her. Once they got some sleep, everything would go back to normal. His gaze fell on the bed once again. Would he get any sleep with her in the same bed, or even the same room? What if she put on that slinky green thing he'd seen in her suitcase? Now, that was a picture—her body outlined by the thin material as she raised her arms to...

"Do you want to use the bathroom, or can I go back in?" she asked.

"What?" He turned to face her. She'd put the flowers down and now stood next to her suitcase, a toothbrush in one hand, toothpaste in the other. "You go ahead."

"It'll just take me a minute to change and brush my teeth." She disappeared into the bathroom and closed the door behind her.

He stared at the door. Change into what? She'd forgotten to take her nightgown in with her. Maybe she wasn't going to wear a nightgown. Maybe she was planning on sleeping in her underwear. If she did, the way he felt now, they'd be doing something other than sleeping tonight.

He rubbed his forehead with his fingertips. What was wrong with him? That woman had ruined his day, his whole weekend. She'd put him in an unconscionable position, forcing him to lie. Why should he suddenly start fantasizing about her?

Wait a minute. Maybe that was the whole idea. What if Kit wanted to seduce him? Those two kisses they'd shared had been pretty potent. She might know that she had that effect on him.

He paced the length of the room and back again. Had she formed some strange fascination with him, without even knowing him? Wait a minute. He stopped pacing. She'd looked so sad during the wedding ceremony. What if she wanted to get married, too? She said not, but it could be a case of protesting too much.

Could it be? It had a kind of horrible logic to it. First she tricks him into pretending they're married, then she steps out of the bathroom in next to nothing. Before he knows it—he *is* married.

He strode across the room to the wooden chair where Kit's case sat propped open. He reached out to grab the tantalizing piece of green material, but snatched his hand back before his fingers actually touched it. If she was trying to tempt him, he needed a counterattack.

He turned, paced the room and ended up in front of the empty closet and stared at the stack of board games. The games—that was it. Nothing could be less romantic than a nice prolonged game of— he grabbed the box on the top and pulled it down—Scrabble, that would do very nicely. He'd offer to let the winner have the bed. He could lose at Scrabble without appearing to throw the game.

He crossed to the bed, knelt on the floor and quickly set the game up in the middle of the quilted bedspread. He'd keep the bed between them, lose the game, then get some sleep while she seethed in frustration in her slip, or her towel, or whatever she'd planned on wearing to this seduction. If she'd planned a trap, she was in for a surprise. This single man would never trade in his bachelorhood for the old ball and chain, no matter what enticements she dangled in front of him.

Kit eyed herself in the bathroom mirror and rapidly finger-combed her hair. She'd have to wait and brush it later. She was taking far too long in here while Ryan waited for his turn, but she'd needed a little breathing space. For a few moments there she'd been caught and held prisoner, just by the way he'd looked at her.

Well, all right, so he wasn't actually looking at her. He'd been staring into space, and she happened to have been standing in that space. But it hadn't felt like that. All afternoon and evening he'd played at the role of bridegroom, taking every possible opportunity to put his arms around her, to touch her neck, cheek, hand, even nuzzle and kiss her. It had probably looked very convincing to Mary and Warren, but she'd felt it for what it was—a deliberate attempt to make her as uncomfortable as possible.

She'd been uncomfortable, all right. Her cheeks were nearly permanently pink from all the times she'd blushed today, thanks to her ridiculously thin skin. But it wasn't until he'd looked at her, with just the two of them alone in the room, that she'd felt as if he'd actually touched her in some quite intimate way.

She dropped her chin down to her chest. Fatigue had finally gotten to her. Imagine her thinking Ryan was interested in her. He only wanted to get out of this ridiculous situation as quickly as possible, just as she did. What she needed was to get some sleep. A good night's rest would make a world of difference.

She gave her robe's sash a good tug. Thank goodness she always left warm nightclothes here. It had been pretty tricky getting them and hiding them in the bathroom without Mary or Warren noticing. They'd have thought it pretty strange for a bride to sleep in a flannel nightgown on her wedding night. She picked up her folded clothes, opened the bathroom door and stepped into the bedroom.

Ryan looked up at her from a kneeling position on the

other side of the bed. What was he doing with a board game? He'd said he was tired.

"What's that you're wearing?" he demanded, rising to his feet.

She glanced down at her robe. Nothing out of place that she could see. She looked back at Ryan. "My bathrobe. What's the matter with it?"

"It looks like a sleeping bag with sleeves."

"So? What are you, an undercover agent for the fashion police? In the dead of winter you don't want glamour, you want warmth. That's what you get with a flannel nightgown and a down-filled robe." She crossed to her suitcase and stowed her clothes. "What are you doing with the Scrabble game?" she asked.

"I thought we'd play... Did you say *flannel* nightgown?"

What was wrong with him? He sounded almost outraged. "Yes, I did. What's the matter, do you have a flannel allergy?" she asked with a toss of her head.

He fixed her with his dark gaze and didn't reply for the longest time. Then the corners of his mouth quirked in a half grin. That had to be a good sign. At least he'd found his sense of humor.

"Flannel and goose down," he said, his gaze sweeping down to her robe's hem and back up to her face. "I'm going to be a little underdressed tonight. I didn't pack for an expedition to Antarctica."

His expression didn't match his light tone, and she found herself tightening the sash of her bathrobe as if he could make it fall from her body with his gaze alone.

"I didn't pack these. We always leave winter clothing here. I snuck in a set of sweats for you, too, in case you need them. I didn't know if you wore pajamas or what."

She was talking too fast, nearly babbling, but he made her so jittery, she couldn't help it.

"Usually I go with 'or what,' but tonight being a special occasion, I'll try the sweats," he said. He didn't move.

Kit played with the end of her robe's sash. Yet another silence stretched out between them. She wasn't going to make it through the next half hour—forget about a whole night—with this tension and awkwardness as constant companions. "You know, it might make it more comfortable for both of us, or at least I know I'd be more comfortable, if we could just act like this is sort of a normal situation."

He rubbed his forehead. "Okay, I'll go for that. How do you propose we 'normalize' our particular situation?"

"I don't know. You must have had some idea about it. You set up Scrabble."

He looked down at the board arrayed on the bedspread. "So I did. All right, how about a game?" He moved to the bed and sat down, stretching one arm along the headboard.

If he could look that relaxed, so could she. She moved to one side of the bed and perched on the edge. "I'm not sure I know how to play the regular way. We always played our own version."

"You and Lindsay? Now, why doesn't that surprise me?"

"And Warren and Mary. In fact, Mary developed the rules. We called it Babble." She lifted the lid of the box and peered inside. "We had a notebook with the rules and words, but it's not in here."

"That's all right. Just tell me how you play, and I'll pick it up."

She reached into the bag of game tiles, blindly chose

one and handed the bag to Ryan. "It's played just like Scrabble, but there's a difference in which words are acceptable."

He pulled out a tile. "So what's acceptable—proper nouns, idioms, things like that?"

"Yes, and made-up words, too." She held up her tile. "I drew a *G*. What did you get?"

"An *A*. I guess I go first." He held out the bag for her to put her tile back. "What kind of made-up words? You mean hyphenated words?" He withdrew his seven tiles and handed the bag to her.

She got her own tiles and lined them up on the stand. "It's hard to explain. We made up our own dictionary of the new words. If I had it I could show you."

Ryan spelled out HEN in the middle of the board. "You're very attached to the Franklins, aren't you?" he asked.

"Naturally. They're like family. The only family I have, actually." She placed a *W* and a *Y* on either side of the *H*. "I get double-letter score for both of my letters. So that's twenty."

He just grunted and studied the letters he'd drawn. There wasn't a score pad in the box, either, so they'd just have to keep track in their heads. She was already fourteen points ahead after just one turn each. If he turned out to be really competitive, this game could make things even more tense than they already were.

"So this whole pretense at being married," he said, his eyes still focused on his rack of lettered tiles, "is simply your crazy idea about protecting them." He carefully placed an *H* and an *A* above her *Y*.

"It's not crazy. I'm doing it for Mary. You know, you only get seven points for that word."

"Is that all?" He drew two letters to replace the two

he'd used and frowned at them. He raised his gaze to meet hers. "You did it for Mary? Because of her heart condition?"

"Yes. Why else would I do such a thing?"

"I can't imagine," he said dryly.

She dropped her gaze and pretended to study her letters. What was he implying? What other reason could she possibly have for doing such an outrageous thing? She hastily put down *A, R, F* after his *H*.

"Harf?" he asked. "What's that?"

"It's the area right in front of a fireplace."

"That would be hearth."

"Yes, but a Dickens character calls it harf, as in 'harf and home.'"

"You're talking about Charles Dickens?"

"Yes, he's one of Mary's favorite writers."

"I see. And how many points do you get for that one?"

"I get twenty, because it's a double-word score."

He narrowed his eyes and looked at the board. "That makes your total, so far, forty, while I have—let's see—thirteen?"

She busied herself drawing her replacement tiles and avoided his gaze. Maybe the game wasn't such a good idea, after all. "You don't have to accept the word. I don't have our dictionary, so I can't defend myself against your challenge."

"No, that's all right. I have my own double-word score here for fourteen points." He used her *R* to spell RIFT. "When do you plan on telling Mary and Warren the truth?"

She glanced up at him. "When? Soon, of course."

"Could you be a little more specific? Soon, as in tomorrow, next week, next year?"

What could she say? She hadn't really thought this part through at all. "Lindsay wanted to have a couple of months for them to get to know Jeff."

"That might work if they lived in some other city. As it is, Mary expects to give us a reception."

"And I told her we didn't want any fuss."

"It's your turn," he reminded her.

She looked quickly at her letters, grabbed a *U* and a *B* and placed them next to his *T*. "I'll call Mary in a couple of days and tell her that it just didn't work out."

He didn't reply, but pursed his lips and studied the board. "How many points did you get for TUB?"

"Eleven. The *B* is on a triple-letter square."

"Okay. I've got BOY—eight points."

"So what do you think?" she prodded.

"About what?"

"My plan to tell Mary."

He raised his eyebrows in mock surprise. "You're actually consulting my wishes? Tell her tomorrow morning."

"I can't."

"Then why ask me? Your turn."

She clamped her lips together. Was he being deliberately maddening? Okay, it was time to show no mercy. She carefully and deliberately placed her *Z* in front of his *Y* and her *G* after it on the triple-word-score square.

"ZYG? I have to challenge that. Not only is it supposed to be spelled with an *i*, but ZIG alone isn't even a whole word."

"Yes, it is. It's how you feel when you have a bad cold in your nose. And, it's a forty-eight pointer."

"I suppose it's in your famous, but missing, dictionary?"

"That's right."

"Then I have my own invented word." He placed his tiles beneath her *G*.

She looked closer to see the word as he laid it out. "GOOM?" she asked.

"Yes, GOOM—a single man who's forced to pretend he's just married someone who makes up her own rules as she goes along."

She stood up. "That's so unfair. I'm not making up the rules. Maybe we'd better stop the game."

He stayed seated on his side of the bed and looked up at her. "Which game do we get to call a halt to?"

"Stop it. You're so, so..." she sputtered.

"Infuriating?"

"Exactly."

"Strange, that's what I would have said about you."

"Me? What did I do?" she protested.

He quirked an eyebrow at her.

"I mean, after the first thing. The marriage part. I've apologized for that. What more can I do?"

"Oh, I don't know. How about calling the whole thing off right now? Wake everyone up and confess. Would Mary have heart failure if you did that?"

The image of Mary, as she'd been earlier in the evening, white-faced and sinking back into her chair, flashed through her mind. "I don't know. I wouldn't want to risk it, and besides, Lindsay would never forgive me."

"Then I'll do it. I don't care if Lindsay never forgives me."

"Play along for Jeff's sake. Please." It had come to this, her practically begging him to keep up a lie. But what else could she do?

He said nothing, and his expression gave nothing away. She could usually read people's faces, but Ryan baffled her. Since they'd been alone she'd had the strangest sensation that he kept expecting something of her, but what it was she couldn't say.

"I'll do it," he said at last. "Not for Jeff, but for you, because it matters so much to you."

"Thank you. I…"

He held up a hand to halt her words. "With the understanding that you'll call Mary and Warren the minute they get back to San Francisco and tell them it's over. More than that, you'll tell them it's an amicable parting."

"I promise."

He stood up slowly and stretched. "I guess I'll get ready for bed myself." He picked up his bag and headed for the bathroom. "You can have the bed," he said over his shoulder. "I'll take the floor." He closed the bathroom door behind him.

Kit stared at the door. Where had that come from? He'd been determined to have the bed. She shook her head. She couldn't figure the man out.

Chapter Four

Ryan turned on the sink's cold tap, cupped his hands to catch the water and splashed it liberally on his face. He nearly yelped from the impact. That wasn't just cold water—it was liquid ice. It figured. Just when he'd wanted to be ready for deep sleep, he'd doused his head with ice water. It fit the pattern of the day.

He lifted his head and stared at the reflection of his dripping face in the mirror. He needed a shave, as usual. He grabbed a towel and mopped up his chin and forehead. There was no point in shaving till morning. His whiskers posed no risk to Kit Kendrick's delicate skin. Miss Kendrick had armored herself with flannel and goose down. Not that she'd needed them, because she'd also protected herself with her own misguided good intentions, and he'd never get past those. And he didn't want to, either. He just wanted out of the entire situation.

He picked up his toothbrush in one fist, the toothpaste in the other, and five times more toothpaste than he needed squirted out onto the bristles. He stared at the toothpaste oozing over both ends of his toothbrush. This was ridiculous. That redhead had him so mixed up, he couldn't even brush his teeth without making a mess.

He carefully washed the excess toothpaste down the drain and set about brushing his teeth. He'd just take it slow and easy. No need to hurry back into the bedroom. He'd give Kit time to get settled in bed. With any luck at all, she'd be asleep, and he wouldn't have to deal with her until morning. In fact, that was a good idea. He'd hang out in here and take his time. She'd looked tired enough to drop off to sleep right away.

He shucked out of his clothes and pulled on the sweatpants Kit had left out for him on the shelf next to the bathtub. Whose sweats were they? Not Warren's. Warren was about his height, and the pant legs on this pair ended a good four inches above his ankles. Now what? It was too cold to sleep on the floor in his shorts. He'd have to go with the sweats. So what if he looked ridiculous? It couldn't be any more absurd than pretending to be married.

He rummaged in his bag for a T-shirt. No sense in even trying to get into the sweatshirt if the pants were this small. He pulled the shirt over his head, gathered up his clothes and bag, and opened the bathroom door.

Kit was sitting in the straight-backed chair. She stood up as he crossed the room.

"I thought you'd be in bed asleep by now," he said, putting down his clothes and suitcase.

"I was waiting for you, because..." Her eyes drifted down to his feet.

He looked down at his feet and back up at Kit. "What is it?"

"Sorry about the pants. I didn't realize that you were so much taller than Jeremy."

"Who's Jeremy?"

"An ex-fiancé."

"An ex-fiancé? You mean yours?" he asked, a sudden vision coming to him of someone else kissing and caressing her the way he had today and Kit responding to that other man, melting into his arms. He gave his head a shake to get the image out of his mind.

"You don't have to sound so stunned," she snapped at him.

"I'm not stunned. From what you said, it sounded like more than one, so I thought you might be talking about Lindsay."

"I know you have an image of me as a spinster desperate to find someone who'll marry me." She flounced across the room to the bed and stripped off the bedspread.

"That's not true," he protested. He followed her to the bed. Good thing she didn't have an inkling of some of the images he'd had of her tonight.

"I'll have you know," she went on as if he hadn't spoken, "that I could be married right now, if I wanted to be." She stripped off the top blanket.

"I believe you. But I don't know why you're so bent out of shape. I'm the one who has to go around looking like a clown in Jeremy's pants."

She paused in her bed-stripping and looked up at him, then down at his bare ankles. A smile threatened to break through. She bit her lip, but her eyes gave her away. "You don't look like a clown at all, more like a toreador." She tossed a blanket at him.

He caught the blanket and held it up in front of him. "Is this for sleeping under or for tantalizing the bulls?"

"We're temporarily out of bulls, I'm afraid. So you'll have to use it for sleeping."

He grabbed up the nearest pillow and scouted out the floor for the best spot.

"Ryan?" Her voice had a tentative catch in it. He looked at her.

"What I said before, about wanting the bed? I wasn't thinking too clearly. You have to drive back to San Francisco tomorrow. It can be dangerous enough driving over the pass in winter without doing it on little or no sleep."

"I won't mind the floor," he said. "I wasn't being too reasonable before, because I was still pretty irritated about this whole fiasco. I'm over that now, and I'd feel like a louse making you sleep on the floor."

"Well, actually," she said, her gaze sliding away from him and back again.

He folded his arms around the blanket and the pillow. Funny thing, he knew that look. He'd met her for the first time maybe eleven hours ago, and her expressions were already familiar. "Now what?" he asked with mock severity. "You want me to sleep in a snowdrift?"

She smiled. "Don't be…" she stopped and bit her lip. "I think we can share the bed. You take that blanket, and I'll take this one." She lifted the second blanket from the bed and wrapped it around her, bathrobe and all. "And you can have the bedspread, too." She lay down on the bed.

"Sounds like a plan." He dropped the pillow back into its place and wrapped the blanket around his shoulders. He gazed at her as she snuggled in her blanket, her red hair spread out on the pillow.

She looked up at him. "Am I taking up too much of the bed? Here, I'll move over." She shifted toward the edge of the bed.

"Don't move. There's plenty of room," he lied, straight-faced. "I'll get the light." He switched off the overhead and felt his way onto the bed in the dark. The mattress bowed under his weight and Kit's well-padded body rolled against his as he settled back onto the pillow.

The darkness enclosed them, and as they stopped rustling the covers of the bed, the perfect silence of the snow-covered night settled around them. Now, at last, he'd get some sleep and forget about the disasters of the day. He could feel Kit holding perfectly still next to him. "You comfortable?" he asked.

"Yes. I'm fine." The silence descended again—then she asked, "Am I crowding you?"

"No, not at all. There'd be more room if the bed was completely horizontal. I think I created a vertical effect when I got in."

"Yes, I think the tilt sign is still lit," she said, and giggled.

Now, that was something he hadn't heard from her. There was nothing quite like the sound of a woman's giggle in the dark. It was a compelling sound, and made him think he'd like to hear her giggle again, maybe even laugh, and then sigh as she pressed her—whoa, he'd better stop right there. What was it about Kit Kendrick that drew him into these erotic fantasies? She'd caused him nothing but trouble, but he kept drifting into these thoughts about her. He shifted restlessly to his side.

"Having trouble sleeping?" Kit asked softly.

"I'm usually out as soon as my head hits the pillow," he said. "But the circumstances are a little unusual."

"I know. I could hardly keep my eyes open, and now I can't get them to stay closed. Maybe we could…" She didn't finish her sentence.

He immediately tensed. Now what was she up to? "Maybe we could what?"

"Talk. Talking in the dark usually makes me sleepy."

He let the tension drain out of his muscles. "Talk. Sure." He waited, but she said nothing. After the silence strung out for a full half minute, he said, "Tell me about Jeremy."

"Jeremy." She sighed.

"Do I hear regret?"

"No. Or at least no regrets about not marrying him. More regret that I let it get so far. He really wanted marriage, and I let him sweep me along into an engagement, even though it wasn't what I really wanted."

"What about the other fiancés? Did they sweep you off your feet, too?"

"There weren't any others. At least, not official ones. After Jeremy I learned how to break it off before it got to that point. But a few of my old boyfriends and some of Lindsay's knew one another, and they would get together sometimes. They called themselves 'The Fiancés,' just for fun."

"A very elite support group."

"More for wounded egos than broken hearts—except, maybe Jeremy. They're mostly all married now."

"And so is Lindsay. That makes you the last holdout."

"Not a bad epitaph." He could hear the smile in her voice.

"Only you'd have to share it with me," he said, smiling in turn.

"Really?" She shifted a little in the bed. He had her interest now. "Why don't you want to get married?"

"It just doesn't fit with my life plan."

"What's a life plan?"

"You don't know? I'd have thought someone like you…" he hesitated. He'd better watch how he put this. She seemed to be sensitive on some issues.

"Yes?" she prompted.

"I understand from Jeff that you've been pretty successful as an industrial designer. That doesn't happen on its own. So, I assumed you had a life plan."

"Maybe I do, only I didn't know it," she said. "Tell me about it. What's your life plan?"

He folded his hands behind his head and stared into the darkness where the ceiling would be, if he could see it. "It's the steps I've taken, and will continue to take, to realize my dream."

"You're really making me pry this out of you, aren't you. Come on, fess up. What's your dream?"

Why had he started this conversation? He never discussed this with anyone. "I'm going to start my own business."

That set up a lot of rustling on her side of the bed. "Really?" she said. She'd rolled onto her side and her voice came directly into his ear. "But you don't have to be single to run your own business."

"Some don't, but I want to get there quickly and without compromising my vision. I've moved around a lot. Each time has meant a big promotion, but moving is hard to do if you're married. Soon I'll have the experience to convince investors that I'm a good risk. Also, I'll have a good bit of capital of my own to put up, because I haven't had to support a wife and family."

"Okay, point taken. But what about when you finally realize all your ambitions, what then?"

"I don't know. I'll see when it happens." He stirred under the blankets. He never really pictured the future beyond the time when he'd made a success of his own company. That part of his life was too hazy and distant to imagine.

"Until then, you're a confirmed bachelor—" she

paused and yawned ''—but I don't imagine that means you're celibate.''

''Well—no,'' he said. This didn't seem the time or place to be discussing his celibacy, or lack thereof. It was about time to shift the focus away from himself. ''What about you?''

She yawned again. ''What about me? Am I celibate?''

''I meant, why don't you want to marry? I assume you're no more celibate than I am.''

''But I am.''

That brought his head right off the pillow. ''What?''

''I said that, unlike you, I'm celibate.''

He lowered his head back onto his pillow. Her statement didn't jibe with his sense of the woman he'd kissed that afternoon. ''But, why?''

She yawned mightily. ''Um, sorry, I can't stop yawning. Why? Simple. I like my independence.''

''I don't see how that's a problem.''

''You don't? Well…'' Her voice drifted off.

''Kit?'' he prompted.

''I don't want to fall in love, because if I do I'll lose my independence. And I'm not going to have sex with someone I don't love, any more than I'm going to marry someone I don't love. So…''

''So you're both single and celibate.''

''Mmm,'' she said, her voice all muzzy. ''Ironic, isn't it? We're two people who plan never to get married, and here we are pretending to have done just that.''

''Ironic, yes, but more than that—unbelievable.'' He rolled onto his side and propped himself up on his elbow. ''I think you're taking this independence thing to an extreme. You're a warm and passionate woman. Why deny yourself what's clearly part of your nature?''

She made no reply. Maybe he'd gotten too personal.

He'd only spoken the truth, but they were virtual strangers. Funny that they could hardly know each other and yet exchange such confidences while lying next to each other in the dark. ''Kit?'' he ventured.

No response. The sound of her breathing came to him soft and steady across the brief dark space between them. She was asleep.

He reached out his arm to shake her and checked himself just in time. Instead, he gripped the bedspread and pulled it over both of them. As he lay back on the pillow, he grinned to himself. It was the first time in his life he'd ever wanted to wake up a woman sleeping in the same bed with him so they could talk.

But she was wrong about herself. They'd talk about it later, maybe tomorrow.

Kit woke to the sound of Ryan's voice and fought without success to open her eyes. She must have drifted off while he was talking, because she'd lost the thread of the conversation. What was he saying? She stopped struggling to force her eyelids open and let his words seep into her brain.

''Kit? I think you'd better wake up. We want to make an early start.''

What? Her eyes snapped open without any effort. The room was bathed in gray morning light. Ryan, fully dressed, but with black hair still wet from his shower, stood by the bed.

''It's morning,'' she said, her voice husky from sleep.

He grinned at her. ''This is real progress. Her eyes are open, and she knows what time of day it is.''

''I thought you were talking to me.''

''I was. I've been talking to you for two minutes, trying to get you to wake up.''

"I mean…" She stopped. She'd fallen asleep while he was talking to her. She could almost recall what he'd been saying. His words hovered tantalizingly on the fringes of her mind.

"I can see you're not a morning person," he said.

She tried to push herself to a sitting position, but the layers of nightgown, bathrobe and blanket hampered her movements. "I hate that phrase. Do I stop being a person just because it's morning?"

His eyes crinkled in a smile. "It describes your preference, not your being."

She wrestled with the blanket until one edge came free and let her sit upright. "But it doesn't. I like mornings very much. I just don't like to leap out of bed and be all active and hearty in the mornings."

Her hair fell over one side of her face, and she finger-combed it with both hands to get it out of the way. What had Ryan been saying last night? It almost came to her. They were talking about marriage….

"Kit?" Ryan said.

She glanced up at him.

"You do have to get a move on if we're going to make it to the airport in time."

"That's all right. I can take the later flight."

"I didn't mean you. Jeff and Lindsay need to catch the early flight to Los Angeles to make their connection to Mexico."

"They're going to Mexico?"

"I know it's confusing, but you might remember that they're the real newlyweds, and they're going to honeymoon in Mexico."

She struggled to get free of the blanket. "You don't have to talk to me like that. I know they're the ones who got married, but no one mentioned a honeymoon." She finally freed herself from the tangled covers and got up from the bed, only to stumble on the hem of her bathrobe. She staggered, trying to get her balance.

Ryan put out a hand to steady her and stopped her just short of careening into his chest. She gazed up into his face and caught the spicy scent of his shaving soap. It came back to her then, everything he'd said last night. She'd heard him, but she'd been too tired to answer. He'd said she was warm and passionate.

He cocked his head to one side. "What is it?"

"What is what?"

"You're looking at me funny."

He'd said it was wrong for her to deny her nature. "Sorry. I just remembered..." She left the sentence unfinished and took a step back, keeping her gaze fastened on his face.

"You just remembered that we're supposed to be married? Good. Did you also remember that we can stop pretending as soon as we get out of here? So why don't you run into the bathroom and get ready? Then we can go downstairs for breakfast together for our last public appearance as newlyweds."

"I can't do that," she said.

"You have to." He consulted his watch. "We have to be out of here in forty-five minutes."

"If you were my real husband, you'd know that I never, ever eat breakfast. No one expects me to do anything but show up in time to leave."

"If I were your real husband, I'd see to it that you reformed your eating habits. Breakfast is the most important meal of the day."

"You know, one day you'll make some lucky woman a terrific mother. Now, run along so I can get ready." She turned away and pretended to busy herself getting clothes out of her bag. The bedroom door clicked softly behind her. She looked over her shoulder. Ryan was gone. Good. It had been too disorienting to have him standing so close to her while his words from last night echoed in her head. If those had been his real words. Maybe she'd dreamed the whole thing.

Kit zipped her traveling bag closed and turned to survey the room. She hadn't left anything behind that she could see, but the bed definitely would not do. It looked like two people had slept in it, but two very separate people—not a honeymoon couple.

She crossed to the bed, pulled the bedspread back and unfurled the blanket she'd cocooned herself in. Just as she spread the blanket on the bed, there was a knock on the door.

Nice of Ryan to knock first, but if anyone saw him they'd think it pretty strange that the new groom had to knock on his own bedroom door.

"Come in," she called.

Mary opened the door partway and peeked in. "Good morning," she said.

"Good morning to you, too," Kit replied, putting as much brightness into her voice as she could. She wasn't ready for a tête-à-tête with the one person in the world who'd always seen right through her. She crossed to the door and opened it wide.

Mary came all the way into the room and folded Kit into a warm embrace. Kit hugged her back.

"Ryan is downing his last cup of coffee and is hurrying Jeff along with him, so I thought I'd pop up here to see you before he whisks you away." She crossed to the straight-backed chair by the window and perched on the edge.

"I'm sorry to rush off like this," Kit said.

Mary waved a hand at her. "You want your privacy. I'd be surprised if you stayed."

Kit moved back to the bed and picked up the second blanket.

"Don't bother with the bed. My housekeeper will see to it."

"Just let me do this part," Kit said, straightening the second blanket on top of the first. Sitting down and facing Mary posed too great a challenge. Yesterday, with everyone else around, was manageable, but on her own she didn't trust herself not to give away the truth.

"I can't tell you how much you surprised me yesterday," Mary said.

Kit picked up the bedspread. Mary had no idea how surprised she'd been herself yesterday to find herself married. "I'm sorry we dropped it like that. I didn't want to tell you that way."

"Don't fret about it. I would have been surprised no matter how gently you broke it to me."

"I must seem as if I don't know my own mind, since I've always made such a big thing about never getting married."

"No, it wasn't that at all. I knew you'd marry when you found the right man. It's just that I always expected that Lindsay would be the one to elope."

Kit froze. "What?" she said before she could stop herself. She turned to face Mary, leaving the spread in a heap on the bed.

"Lindsay's so impulsive. Always has been. She probably would have gotten into even more trouble than she did in her terrible teens if you hadn't been there to stop her."

"Don't give me too much credit. I never stopped Lindsay. I might have slowed her down a couple of times, but that's all.'' And yesterday she hadn't even been able to do that much, but it wouldn't have mattered if she had, because Mary had expected Lindsay to elope. The lies, the pretending, had all been completely unnecessary.

Mary folded her hands in her lap. ''I always pictured giving you a nice wedding—nothing ostentatious, I know you'd hate that, but nice, anyway. Perhaps that's simply because I promised your mother I would.''

Promised her mother? Kit sat down slowly on the end of the bed. ''But you never met my mother. At least not until she was in the hospital, and by then she was in a coma.''

Mary gave a short, self-conscious laugh. ''I suppose you're going to think I'm a little strange, but I've had many conversations with your mother over the years. It seemed to me that being dead was no barrier to worrying about how your child was turning out.''

Kit leaned forward and rested her elbows on her knees. ''What did you talk about?''

''I don't know. Just markers along the way—your getting good grades, your new boyfriends, your summer jobs. The day you won the Langton Prize was a proud one for us, I'll tell you. A four-year full scholarship to Stanford—quite a remarkable achievement. Though you know Warren and I would have gladly paid for your college.''

''I know, but you and Warren paid for quite enough over the years,'' Kit replied quickly. This was old ground between them, and they didn't need to go over it again. ''So you only told her the good stuff, huh? What about the time I got suspended?''

Mary gave her a no-nonsense look. ''We both know that whole escapade was Lindsay's doing, and you took the blame for it so she wouldn't be expelled, because it would have been her third suspension that year.''

Kit could only stare. So Mary had known the truth all along. She really had never been able to get anything past her. Was it possible that she'd succeeded this once? Mary gave no sign that she thought Kit was lying about having married Ryan. She really did have to get out of here as soon as possible, because if Mary hadn't seen through her so far, she would soon enough.

She made a display of looking at her wristwatch. ''Gosh, look at the time.'' She stood up. ''I'm sorry we have to leave so soon. When are you and Warren coming back to San Francisco?''

Mary rose to her feet slowly. ''In a few days. Do you have plans for Friday night? I'd love it if you two could come for dinner. I promise I'll invite only a few close friends, just to introduce Ryan.''

Mary loved to entertain. A few close friends meant a sit-down dinner for twelve. Kit summoned up a smile. ''That would be great. Let me consult with Ryan and let you know.'' By Friday she and Ryan would be safely separated and on the way to divorce.

Mary opened her arms wide and Kit stepped into her embrace. Mary pulled back and held her at arm's length. ''Ryan is absolutely perfect for you. I know you'll be very happy together.''

What could she say to that? She plastered the newly-wed smile on her face again and hugged Mary once more. She'd completely deceived Mary for the first time in her life, but she'd never do it again. Never.

She pulled away from their embrace and looked around the room. ''I think I have everything.'' She picked up her overnight bag. ''Let's go find my husband.''

They made their way downstairs. Ryan was waiting

for them in the front hall, managing somehow or other not to look impatient. He even seemed glad to see her.

"There you are," he said, smiling. "All ready?"

She nodded and dropped her gaze. If he knew that this charade had been completely pointless, he'd be furious— and have every right to be. Guilt was her least favorite emotion, and this morning she had it in spades.

Jeff came in through the front door. She could see Ryan's car sitting in the drive with its trunk open before Jeff closed the door behind him. "Here," Jeff said, reaching for her case, "I'll take that." He disappeared out the front door with it.

Lindsay sailed down the stairs. "Here's your coat," she said, holding out Kit's winter coat.

Ryan took it from Lindsay, held it open for Kit to slip into and trailed his fingers along her jawline as he settled the coat around her shoulders. "Are you okay?" he asked quietly.

She glanced up at him. "Yes, perfect." What was one more lie on top of all the others she'd told this weekend? Ryan had been basically very decent about the whole thing. He hadn't liked it, but he'd played along. She could barely face him, knowing that there'd been no need for the pretense in the first place. Thank goodness for all the bustle of departure. "Are we ready to go?"

Warren emerged from the living room holding a camera. "Don't leave yet. Not before I get you on film."

"Dad," Lindsay moaned, "we don't have time for photography."

"Of course you do," Warren replied. "Come on, let's go outside," he said, and ushered everyone out the front door into the crisp winter morning air.

"Warren takes photographs of every family event,"

Mary explained to Ryan. "We've all come to believe that if it isn't in the family album, then it didn't happen."

Kit hunched her shoulders inside her winter coat. It was horrible to contemplate that this was one event that *hadn't* happened, and it could end up in the album anyway. No, she'd see to it that even if the photo was printed, it would never be placed on those precious pages.

"Stand over there." Warren waved them toward a curve in the front drive where the caretaker's snowblower had recently piled some of last night's snowfall into a tall drift.

They obligingly placed themselves where Warren indicated. He looked at them through the camera's viewfinder while Mary, Lindsay and Jeff stood nearby and watched. Lindsay, in particular, seemed to be enjoying herself. Just wait until she got Lindsay alone and told her what Mary had said—and she'd add a few choice observations of her own, too.

"Kit," Warren called to her, "you look like a suspect in a police lineup. Come on, you're the bride. Let's see a smile."

Ryan slipped his arm around her shoulders and whispered, "Say cheese."

She forced her face into the shape of a smile. If Ryan could be such a good sport, so could she.

Warren clicked the shutter of the camera, then held up one finger, as he always did. "One more, please, just in case. Why don't you kiss your bride, Ryan? That would make a great shot."

Kit stiffened. They could get out of this by pleading shortness of time. But Ryan was already turning her to face him.

"We don't absolutely have to do this, you know," she whispered to him.

"Why not?" he replied quietly. "Besides, I think this is where I came in. You kissed me near this very spot yesterday. Now it's my turn."

He lifted her chin with his fingers and bent his head toward her, watching her all the while. She couldn't hold his intent gaze and closed her eyes to blank out the sight. She'd simply hold perfectly still. After all, they were merely posing for a photograph, and... His lips touched hers, pressing a welcome warmth against her own winter-chilled mouth. He moved his mouth slowly against hers. She leaned toward him, suddenly, inexplicably yearning for more.

He slid his hand from her chin to the back of her head and wrapped the other arm around her waist, but she hardly needed to be held closer, because she was already pressing closer herself, slipping her hands inside his open coat and placing her palms flat against his chest. The heat of his skin seeping through the wool of his sweater matched the warmth of his mouth against hers. And still it wasn't enough.

"Okay, you two," Warren called. "You can break it up now. I've used up all the film."

Ryan lifted his head, breaking their kiss, but still held her tightly. Kit opened her eyes and blinked slowly. What had happened to her? She'd forgotten what she was doing.

"See? What did I tell you?" Ryan said, smiling down into her face with all his dark-eyed handsomeness. "You're too warm and passionate to live a celibate life."

Chapter Five

Kit scanned the airport monitor for her flight number. Wonder of wonders—her flight was on time. Airport maintenance crews must have managed to clear the snow from all the runways. That was a lucky break, because she'd had all she could take of Lindsay and Jeff's company. During the entire trip into Reno they had kept up a running commentary, some of it borderline ribald, on Ryan's and her unplanned "honeymoon."

"Everything okay?" Ryan's voice came from just behind her.

She focused on the monitor one last time, even though she'd just read it, because everything was not okay, from the first needless lie to the last breathtaking kiss. But she couldn't tell Ryan that. She turned slowly to face him. "Flight's right on time."

"Guess you'll be glad to get out of here," he said, and glanced meaningfully toward Jeff and Lindsay, who were standing in the check-in line for their flight to Los Angeles.

"Yes," she said briefly. She owed him a large-sized apology for dragging him through the pretend marriage, but couldn't seem to get the words out.

"I've been thinking," he said. "You don't have to fly back. You could cash in your ticket and drive back with me."

Oh, no, she couldn't. That would not be at all advisable. She was too distracted just thinking about that circuit-erasing kiss. How would she handle being alone in a car with him for four hours? "Thanks for offering, but my airport's at the car—I mean, my car's at the airport. And, anyway—" she raced on "—I'll get home sooner if I fly."

Lindsay came sailing toward them, leaving Jeff to stand in the check-in line. "I almost forgot. My ring, I need my ring back."

Kit glanced down at her left hand. She'd forgotten all about Lindsay's wedding ring. She grabbed the ring firmly and tugged. It didn't move even a fraction of an inch. "I can't get it off."

"What do you mean? You have to get it off. I can't go on my honeymoon without my wedding ring."

"Come on, Lindsay," Ryan said. "No need to be so dramatic."

Lindsay rolled her eyes. "Men," she said to Kit, "they simply don't understand, do they."

Kit twisted the ring from side to side. With effort she could make it move around but not upward and off her finger. She shook her head. "It's stuck."

"It can't be stuck," Lindsay insisted. "It just can't be. You got it on, didn't you? So you have to be able to get it off."

"Maybe some soap and cold water will do the trick,"

Kit said. She looked around and spotted a ladies' room. "I'll just duck in there for a minute and see."

"I'll come with you," Lindsay said.

She didn't want Lindsay's help. Lindsay was already nearly making a scene. She glanced at Ryan.

"No, Lindsay," Ryan said. "You'd better stay here in case your flight is called."

Lindsay wavered long enough for Kit to move off. She hurried into the ladies' room and made straight for the soap dispenser. Some nice slippery soap should do the trick. She pumped the dispenser several times and squirted pink liquid soap into her palm. She worked it all around the ring and her finger. The ring slid smoothly one-half inch upward and jammed.

She stared at the foaming circle of gold. This couldn't be happening to her. The ring had to come off. Lindsay's hysterics aside, she couldn't go to work tomorrow wearing a wedding ring. Maybe cold water would shrink her finger. She ran the water from the cold tap over her hand and counted to thirty as her hand slowly went numb.

"It's Kit Kendrick, isn't it?" a woman's voice said from behind her.

Kit jerked her head up and stared in the mirror. The reflection of Emmaline Godfrey smiled at her. Of all the horrible luck to run into someone who knew her. She grabbed a handful of paper towels and twisted her face into something like a smile. "Emmaline, fancy meeting you here." Something niggled at the back of her mind. Emmaline was an old friend of Mary and Warren's, but something else, too. "Are you coming or going?"

"Just arrived. And you?" Emmaline's gaze darted from Kit's hands to her face and back to her hands.

Kit continued with her elaborate drying of her hands,

keeping a towel over her ring finger the entire time. "Just this minute leaving."

"I was in there," Emmaline gestured to a toilet cubicle behind her, "and I heard the water running and running, and I thought, goodness, that person must be from out of state to let the water run like that. And then I find it was you."

"Well I, for one, don't think that water conservation is more important than hygiene, do you?" Kit said.

"No, well, I..." Emmaline stammered.

Emmaline probably thought she was completely nuts, but that was better than her thinking she was married. Her hands felt raw from rubbing with the towel. She turned slightly away from Emmaline, slipped her left hand into her coat pocket and tossed the used towels into the trash with her right.

"I have to dash. They just called my flight." Kit moved toward the door, and it came back to her. Emmaline's daughter-in-law was Pam Saget, the social news columnist for the *San Francisco Star*. She risked one backward glance. Emmaline was watching her with narrowed eyes. But she hadn't seen the ring. She couldn't have.

Kit hurried down the corridor to rejoin Ryan and Lindsay. Good thing the airport was jammed with travelers this morning. Emmaline would never find her in this crowd. Even so, she had to get out of here, and fast. If only she could get this stupid ring off her finger.

"Well?" Lindsay asked as Kit approached.

Kit shook her head. "I'm sorry. Nothing seems to work."

Ryan took her hand and inspected her finger. "You can have it cut off when you get home."

"Ryan, what a horrible thing to say," Lindsay said.

"Even as a joke, the idea of cutting off someone's finger is gruesome."

"I wasn't joking, and I didn't mean her finger," Ryan said, exchanging a look with Kit. "I was talking about the ring."

"The ring? Cut *my* wedding ring? No, you can't do that. Here, Kit, let me see it. I'll get it off. You probably just need another person to pull on it." Lindsay made a grab for Kit's hand, but Ryan held on to it.

"Leave her alone." Ryan's voice had an edge to it that Kit hadn't heard before. "She's done her best, and it looks sore to me. There's no point in Kit injuring herself. I don't think it's going to come off."

He looked down at her hand in his rather large one and rubbed his thumb gently over her reddened finger.

Jeff trotted up to them, panting slightly. "Hey, Lindsay, we're all checked in and we have to go. Our gate's at the other end."

"We can't go. Kit still has my ring. She says it's stuck."

Kit gritted her teeth. Lindsay was at her most impossible. She'd like to get her alone and tell her to shape up.

"If it's stuck, it's stuck," Jeff said with a shrug. "We'll get it when we return from Mexico."

"But what if she has to have it cut off?"

"I'll buy you a new one. Come on, Lindsay, we have to go. We're married, that's all that matters. Who needs a ring?"

Lindsay blinked at him and her face cleared. She gave him one of her radiant smiles. "I love you, Jeffrey Sanderson."

"Same here, Mrs. Sanderson. Now, let's go." Jeff stuck out a hand to Ryan. "Bye. Thanks for everything, especially, you know…"

Ryan released Kit's hand and shook Jeff's. "I know. Forget it. Have a happy honeymoon."

Lindsay hugged Kit. "I'm sorry, Kit. I'm a brat. I know it. I'm so lucky to have a friend like you. You should get married. It's wonderful."

Kit returned the embrace. How like Lindsay to behave outrageously and then repent the next instant. "I'm glad you're happy, but you know me. This is as close as I'll ever get to marriage."

Lindsay shook her head. "Don't say that. You never know what might happen." She turned and gave Ryan a brief hug and peck on the cheek. And Jeff did the same to Kit.

Both Jeff and Lindsay looked entirely happy. They set off down the wide corridor, but after a few steps, Lindsay ran back and whispered in Kit's ear, "Promise me you won't cut off my ring. Or at least promise you'll wait until I get back, please."

"I'll try," Kit said. She wasn't going to promise anything about the ring. She could just picture herself walking into work tomorrow wearing it. She'd never hear the end of it. Lindsay gave her a pleading look, then turned and hurried off to join Jeff.

"She doesn't want you to cut off the ring. Right?" Ryan asked, frowning.

"When I was twelve I got a scholarship to the Elizabeth Woods School. Everyone wore a uniform, but everyone still knew who the scholarship girls were. You can never know the full meaning of being alone until you're a gawky kid with bright red hair in a room full of girls who're all talking to one another and very deliberately not talking to you."

"Was Lindsay there?"

"She walked in, instantly saw what was going on and came over and talked to me."

"For that you're grateful to her forever after."

"No. For that I'll love her forever after. She's impulsive. Sometimes she's thoughtless. But she can also be incredibly generous. Besides, she's as close as I'll ever get to having a sister. Do you love your sisters less because they're not paragons?"

Ryan didn't reply but gazed at her silently instead. Something about his look was thoughtful, assessing. She'd wanted to give him another perspective on Lindsay, but she'd revealed more about herself than she'd intended. She looked at her watch. "I'd better go. My plane will be boarding soon."

"Okay, I'll walk you to the security check."

Together they headed toward the checkpoint where passengers and well-wishers parted company. Now what would she say? It's been great pretending to be married to you? There wasn't anything in the etiquette books to cover this situation. He'd been nice about it, all things considered. Maybe she should thank him. But really, Lindsay and Jeff were the ones who owed him thanks.

They arrived at the conveyer belt with its X-ray camera next to the electronic doorway for scanning passengers. Kit turned to Ryan. "This is it. You'd better be on your way before it starts snowing again."

"The weather report said clear skies."

"Yeah, I know. That's what it said yesterday, too."

"Point taken. Are you going to be all right? I mean, with the ring?"

"Sure. It'll probably fall off just as soon as I get home. No problem."

"Don't hurt yourself, that's all."

"I won't."

People were moving around the two of them to get to the conveyer belt. It was time to go, and she wanted nothing more than to get out of here, so what was this strange reluctance? "I'd better go. I don't want to miss my plane since you got me up in time to catch it."

"Kit?"

"Yes?"

He hesitated, then said, "Take care."

Funny, it felt as if he'd meant to say something else. "Sure," she replied. "You, too." She moved into line and put her carry-on case on the conveyer belt. "See you at work tomorrow," she said over her shoulder.

He smiled and waved. She walked through the scanning portal, picked up her carry-on case and walked to her gate without looking back. She went through the boarding routine and slipped into her seat with a sigh. It was over, at last. The past day and night must have been the longest twenty-four hours of her life.

Come Wednesday, she'd phone Mary and tell her that she and Ryan had made a mistake. How should she put it? There were no hard feelings on either side, but neither one of them wanted to be married—not really. They were just friends. That "just friends" bit always sounded weak. But she'd promised Ryan not to say anything to put him in a bad light, and she wouldn't want to, anyway. So she'd say they were good friends, that would soothe Mary. Maybe. Mary had been pretty sold on Ryan. She might try to talk Kit into trying again. No, she'd hold firm. She'd say it was over, and that was it.

The flight attendant stopped by Kit's seat and gestured to her seat belt. Kit snapped it on and gave it an additional tug to tighten it. It would be a good idea to plan her speech to Mary ahead of time, that way she wouldn't fall into any traps. How she hated lying, especially to Mary. This would put an end to all of it.

She let her head fall back on the seat and closed her eyes. Instantly, an image of dark eyes in a handsome face appeared. He was smiling, and then he bent his head close to hers and... She snapped her eyes open and felt a familiar warmth steal up her neck. Ryan had sneaked into her subconscious somehow. Not a good sign at all. Whenever that had happened before, the man always ended up wanting to marry her. It was a strange phenomenon. Almost as if once he'd taken up residence in some part of her mind, he felt it incumbent on him to move in physically—lock, stock and wedding ring.

The ring, why did she have to remind herself? She'd automatically folded her right hand over her left when she'd sat down. Now she lifted her right palm and peeked underneath. She'd really done a number on her finger trying to get the ring off. If Emmaline Godfrey hadn't turned up, she might have found the right combination of ingredients to liberate the ring. As it was, her finger was still pink and a little swollen from all the twisting and tugging, and the gold circle was still snugly in place.

Ryan had been sweet to defend her against Lindsay. He'd stroked her finger so gently. He had wonderful hands, large and strong. She shifted in her seat, crossing and recrossing her legs. There she went again, thinking about him. Too bad he was going to work at Calvert. She'd be bound to see him. Well, she'd be polite, but not overly friendly. He'd get the message.

Ryan swung a left and slowed his car to enter the Calvert Container Corporation parking lot. He was early, but the parking lot was already more than half-full. Most of the cars had to belong to the shift workers in the plant, but some of them were executives' cars. John Calvert had warned him in his last interview that everyone in the company had a strong work ethic. Ryan had assured him that he did, too, and it seemed like a good idea to back up his words by coming early and staying late.

He pulled into a parking place not too far from the entrance to the corporate offices. The early morning fog wisped around the building and obscured the neighboring warehouses. When he got out of his car, a damp chill laden with marine odors from the bay wrapped itself around him. He buttoned his suit jacket and hurried into the building.

The dark-haired receptionist didn't recognize his face. "May I help you?" she inquired.

"I'm Ryan Holt," he told her.

"Oh, *you're* Ryan Holt," she said with a brilliant smile, as if his name rang a definite bell for her. "Mr. Calvert said you knew the way to your office."

"That's right. I'm all set."

"Good. And congratulations," she said with another flash of white teeth. "I hope you'll be very happy."

"Thanks," he said. Ryan glanced at her nameplate— Nina Smith. He'd remember her name, too, after such a warm welcome.

A few people with unfamiliar faces passed him as he made his way to his new office. Maybe Kit's office was on this side of the building, and he'd run into her. They hadn't worked out any agreement about how to act around each other. It would be pretty silly to pretend they were complete strangers, but then what if someone asked them to explain how they'd met? No one knew about Jeff and Lindsay's wedding. They should get their stories straight first.

On the other hand, they might not encounter each other

at all, because they worked in different divisions. He slowed his steps. He hadn't considered that possibility. In fact, he'd counted on seeing her today. It was his first day. With Jeff honeymooning, Kit was the only person he knew here.

She'd been on his mind the entire drive back from Tahoe yesterday. It would have been nice to have her along. He'd nearly asked her again to cash in her ticket and drive back with him, but she'd seemed to want to get back early.

He looked in every office on his way to his own, but didn't spot her. He'd just walked into the office he'd been assigned during his last visit here, when Len Bergman appeared in the doorway.

"You're here bright and early. Good for you." Fiftyish and heavyset, Len Bergman gave off an air of gruff bonhomie. He was the senior analyst for production and would be working closely with Ryan.

"Seen anyone yet? No?" Len answered his own question. "Well, let me be the first to offer my congratulations." He pumped Ryan's arm up and down several times.

"Thank you," Ryan said. He'd thought all along that there had been some heavy competition for the job. Apparently, it had been stiffer than he'd realized.

"I was a little surprised, as you can imagine," Len went on. "But I'm really happy for you."

"Thanks," Ryan said again with a little less enthusiasm. Len had been surprised? Someone else must have been the first-choice candidate. He'd just as soon not have known about it, but he had the job, and that was all that mattered. "I'm happy to be here, and I'm eager to start."

Len's smile faltered slightly, then broadened. "I see that you already have the Calvert spirit. Good for you."

Ryan's gaze drifted down to his desk. A pile of papers rested on the top and the message light on his phone was blinking. He'd really have to hit the ground running if he wanted to keep up.

He glanced up and found Kit standing in his doorway. She looked terrific in a dark green suit. He smiled at her. She smiled weakly back, her eyes darting nervously from him to Len.

"Excuse me," she said. "I'm sorry to interrupt, but could I have a word with you, Ryan?"

"I can see that I'm not needed," Len said, backing out the doorway as Kit slid by him. "Best wishes to you, Kit. I know you two will be very happy."

Ryan blinked. "What?"

"No, please," Kit said. "There's been a misunderstanding."

"Already?" Len gave a hearty laugh. "Well, I'll leave you two to work it out. Give me a call if you need anything, Ryan." He left and closed the door behind him.

Ryan folded his arms across his chest. "Did he mean what I think he meant?"

Kit took a step closer. "I'm sorry. I'm really sorry."

"He was congratulating me. I thought it was for getting this job." He put his fingers to his temple. "Wait a minute. The receptionist congratulated me, too. How many people did you tell?"

"I didn't tell anyone. Honest. Someone saw me in the ladies' room at the airport trying to get Lindsay's wedding ring off." Kit held up her left hand. The ring finger was swathed in bandages.

"What happened to your finger?"

"Nothing. I just couldn't get the ring off, so I thought I'd cover it up."

"So someone who works here saw you with a wedding ring and put two and two together."

"She doesn't work here. She has no connection to Calvert. She's a friend of Mary and Warren's, and she's Pam Saget's mother-in-law." She paused.

"And now you're going to tell me who Pam Saget is?"

"Please don't be mad."

"Too late. Who is she?"

"The society page editor for the *San Francisco Star*."

He dropped his hands to his sides and stared at her. "Are you telling me that there was an announcement in the morning paper?"

"It was an item." Kit held up a thumb and forefinger half an inch apart. "A very short item, in her column."

"Not, apparently, short enough. Does everyone here know about the item?"

"Only those people who've picked up their voice mail. Nina put out a company-wide announcement."

Ryan turned and eyed the blinking light on his phone. "Great, just great." He marched over to his phone, picked up the receiver and looked up at Kit. "I don't know the phone system here yet. How do you send out a broadcast message?"

"What are you going to say?"

"What do you think?"

"Please, don't." She followed him to his desk as if she would try to physically stop him if he touched the dial.

He gazed at her worried face and let the receiver slip back into the cradle. "Why?"

She sighed. "If we act like it's a big deal, everyone

will expect us to demand a retraction from the paper. Then Mary and Warren will hear about it.''

"Are you proposing that we continue to pretend that we're married?''

"No, of course not,'' she answered quickly. "Let's just tell people one by one that it's not true. Treat it lightly. We could say it's a misunderstanding. As soon as they see we don't have anything to do with each other, they'll drop it.''

He rested his palms flat on the desk and leaned toward her. "That line isn't going to be too convincing, since we've just been closeted in my office with the door closed.''

Kit glanced around at the door and back at Ryan. "I guess that doesn't look too good, does it.''

He straightened and folded his arms. "I guess not.''

She chewed on her lower lip and fiddled with the bandages on her ring finger.

"So, do you think that maybe we should open the door? That would give us an opportunity to tell everyone that we barely even know each other.'' He sounded more ironic than he really meant to be, but Kit was being uncharacteristically quiet. Why didn't she talk back to him, the way she had over the weekend?

Kit's gaze slid away from his and back again. That look again. She was up to something.

"What is it, Kit?'' He put a warning note into the question.

"I got a message for both of us on my voice mail. It's from John.''

"John? As in John Calvert, president and CEO, et cetera?''

"Mmm.'' She studied her toes.

"He wants to congratulate us on our marriage? Well,

maybe it's just as well. If we have to start disillusioning people, we might as well start at the top. Right?''

''I think it will be fine if we tell him right away that we're not married. Just march in there and tell him.'' Her tone of voice didn't match the conviction of her words.

Ryan felt a peculiar feeling in his midsection, somewhat like the downward plunge of a roller coaster from its highest peak. A sickening feeling, really, made worse by the knowledge that there was no stopping and getting off before the end of the ride.

Chapter Six

Kit sank into the client's chair in front of John Calvert's desk. She should have known that gossipmonger, Emmaline Godfrey, wasn't to be trusted from the first moment she saw her at the airport. Now here she was having to explain away her "marriage" without creating a stir that would somehow get back to Mary and Warren. Maybe if she got the right tone of laughing incredulity when she told John that it was all a misunderstanding, he'd buy it without wanting further details.

From the corner of her eye she watched Ryan take the other client's chair. He looked too grim. If he kept on taking it so seriously, everyone would wonder why he wasn't demanding a retraction from the paper.

John himself waited until they were both seated before taking his own, larger chair. With its high back, black leather upholstery and rich wood trim, his chair told everyone in the room who had the advantage of rank. Not that John needed any external accoutrements. He had only to beetle his extremely bushy eyebrows at someone and jut his large chin forward, just as he was doing right now, to send the message of his power.

John folded his hands and rested them in front of him on the desk. "I understand congratulations are in order."

"They're not," Kit said right away. "We were mistaken for another couple." She bit her lip. Maybe she shouldn't have mentioned the other couple. What if John asked who they were? She glanced over at Ryan and held her breath.

John raised his eyebrows at Ryan in a silent query.

"We met for the first time this weekend. We're not married," Ryan said.

Kit let her breath out. She would thank him later for not explaining. They simply had to wait until the day after tomorrow when she could tell Mary and Warren the marriage was over.

"I see," John said. "I'm glad to hear it."

"So are we," Kit said on a breathy laugh.

"You should know," John said, "that I'm not in favor of married couples working for the same company. Conflicts at home can spread to work and vice versa."

"Of course, that wouldn't have been a problem for us," she said with another laugh.

John raised his impressive eyebrows at her.

Why had she said that? It had just popped out of her mouth. "I mean, we don't work in the same department. Our offices are at opposite ends of the building. Not that it matters, because we're not married. We hardly know each other." Why couldn't she just shut up? She was only making it worse.

"In the past, that would have been the case," John said, "but no longer. We brought Ryan into the company because of his experience with newer organizational styles. He's going to lead the way in putting an end to our over-the-wall methods of communication.''

'''Over the wall'? It sounds like a prison breakout,'' Kit said, looking back and forth from John to Ryan.

"It's the way many American companies operate,'' Ryan said. "One department works on a project, then, in a manner of speaking, tosses it over the wall to another department. There's no cooperative discussion or play of ideas.''

"We're changing that practice here,'' John said. He paused and looked first at Ryan, then at Kit. "Starting with your departments—which is why I place a great deal of importance on your getting along both professionally and personally.''

"What?'' Kit said.

John went into his eyebrow thing again. She should have kept her mouth shut.

Ryan leaned forward in his chair. "I'm sure we'll work together very well.''

John looked at her. It was her turn. "I see no problem,'' she lied.

"Just what I'd hoped you'd say,'' John said. "Because we have a potential client coming on Wednesday, and I want the two of you to convince them to go with us.''

"Wait a minute. Why us? Isn't that the sales department's job?'' Kit asked.

John nodded. "Normally, but Arthur and Harriet Winston are a couple of mavericks. They do things their own way, and their way has been very profitable. They're going public at the end of the year.''

"I've heard of them,'' said Ryan. "They have a mail order business, right?''

"Yes, Mom and Popcorn. AGC had their container

contract, but the Winstons aren't happy about the price or the product. We'll convince them we can do better.''

''I don't know about Ryan,'' Kit said, ''but I don't have any experience in sales.''

''The Winstons refuse to talk to our sales staff. They want to meet the people who will be responsible for the actual production. That's how they do business. So you two need to come up with something that will persuade them to go with us.''

''By Wednesday?'' Kit said. It wasn't really a question, more of an appeal to reason. But John simply nodded in affirmation and placed his hands flat on the desk, a signal that he was going to stand up.

Kit jumped to her feet before John was fully upright. Ryan followed her lead. This business with the Winstons sounded like a lot of work in too short a time. But, looking on the bright side, the question of their not being married seemed settled. She could have said less, but John believed them, and that was the important thing.

''As I've told you before, Ryan, I'm very happy to have you with the company,'' John said.

Ryan smiled. ''Thanks, I'm happy to be here.''

Kit shifted her feet. Time to break up this society of mutual happiness and get out of here. ''Guess we'll be getting back to work.''

John smiled and nodded, then his gaze shifted to Kit's left hand. ''What happened to your finger?''

''My finger?'' She looked down. Good grief, she'd been picking at the bandage without realizing it. A two-inch strip of tape dangled from her finger, and the entire gauze wrapping was in danger of coming loose. She plastered the tape back in place and held her hand up for inspection. ''You mean this? I injured my hand, but it's fine, really.''

No sooner were the words out than she felt the heat of a blush rushing up her neck. He'd caught her off guard, and now she looked like the worst liar in the world, which she was. She had to get out of John's office fast.

"I appreciate your taking the time to check out this rumor," she said, edging toward the door.

"If you *had* gotten married, I would certainly have offered you my congratulations. But since you *didn't*, I'm very glad," he said, escorting them to the door.

She laughed as if he'd made a great joke, and nearly dived out of the room as soon as the door was open. He'd put such a strange emphasis on his words. What had he meant by it? Maybe Ryan would have some idea—not that they could talk here. John's assistant, Lorraine, wasn't at her desk, but she couldn't be far away.

"Let's go to my office," she said to Ryan.

No sooner were the words out of her mouth than Lorraine came through the door. She was a grandmother five times over, although with her slim figure and blond bob, she didn't look it. She'd always been after Kit to get married and have children. "There you are, Kit," Lorraine said. "I was afraid I was going to miss you. I'm so happy for you." She hugged Kit. "I'm Lorraine," she said to Ryan over Kit's shoulder.

"Kit and I aren't married," Ryan said. "But I'm pleased to meet you, anyway." Lorraine released Kit from her embrace and frowned. "What?"

"It's true," Kit said.

"But it was in the newspaper," Lorraine protested.

"You know what they say about believing everything you read," Ryan said with a smile.

"You couldn't find a better wife than this one," Lorraine said to Ryan.

"Lorraine, please," Kit said. Was every encounter going to be this embarrassing?

"I'm sure you're right," Ryan said easily, "but it so happens neither one of us wants to get married."

Lorraine put her hands on her hips. "You're just going to live together? What about children?"

"No! We're not living together, either," Kit said a little too loudly. This was the most exasperating situation she'd ever been in. "We hardly even know each other. It's all a big misunderstanding."

Lorraine stared at her wide-eyed. "Well, excuse me."

"Sorry to run off, Lorraine," Ryan said, moving toward the door. "But this is my first day, and I've already been assigned to work on a new product with Kit." He fixed Kit with a meaningful look, his mouth grim. "You wanted to show me something about that assignment, I believe?"

Kit grabbed at the escape route he offered. "Yes. It's in my office. Bye, Lorraine." She'd soothe Lorraine's feelings later. Right now she had to get out of here. The hallway was blessedly empty. She signaled Ryan to follow her and hurried toward her office.

With a wave of her hand, she shooed him into her office and closed the door without anyone seeing them. Ryan faced her, his jaw set, his gaze angry. Maybe they'd be better off with the door open. No, she had to face the music sometime.

"I'm sorry," she said.

"That's what you said before," he replied. "But your apologies don't seem to affect the general impression that we're married."

"I know. It's awful."

"Awful? It's not your first day of work here. I'm supposed to be showing what I can do in this job, which is stressful enough in itself without having to constantly deny published reports of my marriage.''

''I hate it, too, but we only have to tell a few more people. Then they'll tell everyone else, and it'll be over. I think if we treat it lightly, make a joke of it...''

''Make a joke?'' Ryan interrupted her. ''The way you did when Lorraine suggested we were living together?''

''Lorraine took me by surprise. I'll be better prepared the next time. I thought I pulled it off really well with John.''

''Right. Especially when you told him you'd injured your finger. You looked as guilty as sin.''

''I can't help it. I'm not used to lying, and I get all red in the face unless I've thought it all out ahead of time.''

''If you'd just had the damn ring cut off, you would have been infinitely more believable.'' He gestured at her hand. ''That ridiculous bandage makes it look like you're hiding something. I mean, who ever hurts the ring finger on their left hand?''

He had every right to be angry at her, more than he even knew. She gulped and turned away from him. Why had she listened to Lindsay? The whole situation was a big mess, and a great deal of the blame belonged to her.

''I'll go out on my lunch hour and take care of it.'' Her voice was husky, and she had to clear her throat. She looked down at her hand. The tape had come undone again, and she tried to stick it back in place.

''Kit, I'm sorry.'' He came up behind her and, taking her by the shoulders, turned her to face him.

She glanced up at him and then quickly back down at her fingers. Ryan angry was hard to take, but Ryan apologizing and giving her the full force of his dark gaze made her feel a little shaky. "No apology is necessary. You have every right to be angry."

"I guess I do, but when you look like you're about to cry, it makes me feel like maybe I don't."

Now she did look at him. "Me, cry?" she said.

"I know," he said with a grin, "'don't be silly.'" He took her left hand in both of his and inspected the bandage. "I think this tape has had it."

"I should've brought some more with me, just in case." She let her hand rest in his. Surprising how gentle his touch was, and how comforting.

"It's pretty loose," Ryan said, testing the fit of the bandage. "I'll help you rewrap it." He tugged on the remaining tape and the whole dressing came off.

Kit's hand, with the ring finger now exposed, rested in the cradle of his palm. It felt nice, too nice. "That's all right. I can fix it." She moved to pull her hand away, but he closed his fingers and imprisoned it.

"Let me help. It's probably harder to manage it one-handed." He unclasped his hand and peered at her finger. "It's even more swollen than it was yesterday. Maybe you'd better go get it cut off right now."

"It's not the ring's fault. My finger was fine until I tried some extreme measures to get the ring off this morning, and my dumb thin skin reacted by getting all puffy."

He bent over her hand, his head at a level with hers and so close, she could touch his cheek with her lips if she leaned just slightly forward. He turned his head and met her gaze. His own eyes darkened as if he could read her mind and approved of her notion.

"You have exquisite skin," he murmured. "The softest I've ever felt."

Kit's heart raced triple-time. She should move, break

contact, anything but stay within inches of Ryan's lips. This was crazy, but nice crazy.

The knock at the door registered in one corner of her brain, but that part of her brain had disengaged from the rest of her. Somehow, standing within a breath of Ryan's mouth and being trapped into immobility by his hungry gaze consumed all her will.

The door opened without her invitation, and Cynthia, Kit's assistant, popped her head in. "Oh, my gosh" was all Cynthia managed to get out, but it was enough to reconnect Kit's brain to her body.

Kit jerked her head away from Ryan's. Ryan himself straightened and turned to gaze at Cynthia, who goggled at them both from the doorway.

"Sorry," Cynthia squeaked. "I thought... Lorraine said..." She gasped, staring at Kit's hand still resting in Ryan's. "Congratulations and best wishes and all that. Sorry." She retreated, pulling the door closed.

"Cynthia, wait," Kit called. Too late. She jerked her hand away from Ryan's and snatched at the gauze bandage he still held in his other hand. "Give me that." This man had a very bad effect on her, and she was going to put a stop to it right now.

"Let me help," he said, reaching to take it back.

"You've helped enough, thank you very much. I'll do it myself." She moved out of his reach. How had she let herself get into this situation? She'd been about to kiss him, of all things. Even if he hadn't moved those few centimeters, she would have. With shaking hands she wound the gauze around her finger. In some other situation, she could see giving into impulse. But how could she have forgotten that theirs wasn't an ordinary situation?

He raked his fingers through his hair. "What did I do?"

"Nothing, only provided a spectacle for Cynthia to go running around gossiping about."

"Me? What about you?"

Yes, what about her? What could she have been thinking? But with Ryan standing so close, it had been hard for her to think. Even now it was hard to concentrate. She turned to him. "Why don't you just go back to your office?"

"I'd like nothing better." The irritation in his voice matched her own.

"Good," she snapped back. "And if you don't mind, please keep to your side of the building so that we don't have to see each other."

"That might be a little hard since we're supposed to be working on a project together." He didn't trouble to keep the irony out of his voice.

"We can E-mail each other. We don't have to meet face-to-face."

He marched to the door and rested his hand on the doorknob. "Suits me."

"Me, too." She crossed to her desk and ripped some cellophane tape from the dispenser on her desk.

"Fine," he said, opening the door.

"Fine," she said, jamming the tape onto her re-wrapped finger.

"You're probably one of those irritating people who has to have the last word, aren't you?" he said from the doorway.

She set her jaw. "Funny, that's what I would have said about you."

Their gazes locked for a moment, then he moved through the doorway and closed the door behind him.

What an impossibly irritating man. Could she really have been tempted to kiss him?

Ryan hurried down the hall to Kit's office, clutching a sheaf of papers in his hand. He was going to put a stop to her obstructionism right now. He'd been given the mission of ending over-the-wall project planning at Calvert, but somehow Kit had managed to erect the equivalent of the Great Wall of China between them.

Her office door was open, and Kit herself stood by a drafting table gazing down at what looked like specs. She wore a blue suit today and looked nice. But then, she always looked good. Even bundled in flannel and goose down she'd looked terrific. But her looks weren't going to buy her any slack from him. Not today.

He waited in the doorway a moment, but she didn't notice him. That was one of the many differences between them. He'd know if she was nearby.

He tapped on the open door. "Knock, knock. May I come in for a moment? There are a few things we need to talk over."

She jerked around and stared at him. Her cheeks went pink and her chin jutted out. That was Kit, all right—an unlikely combination of vulnerable and tough, and he had to admit that it got to him. But not this time. She wasn't going to get around him with her ready blushes, and she wasn't going to rile him with her antagonism.

"I prefer not to meet in person," she said. "I thought I made that clear yesterday."

He closed the door and leaned against it. "You did, but—" he waved the sheaf of papers at her "—your alternative isn't working."

She gestured with her chin to the papers he held. "What's that?"

He waved the papers in the air. "This represents the sum total of our E-mail exchange. I printed out everything, and it adds up to zip." He crossed to where she stood and tossed the papers on the table in front of her. "You've negated every suggestion I've made. With less than twenty-four hours to go, I think you'll agree that we need a new approach."

She glanced down at the papers and back up at him. "All right."

He stared at her. "Did you say 'all right'?"

"You heard correctly." With brisk motions, she gathered up the E-mail printouts and tossed them in the wastebasket. Then she assembled the papers she'd been looking at when he came in and waved him to a table by the window.

He sat down slowly in the chair she indicated. What was she up to? He'd expected a lot of different reactions, but not cooperation.

"I think it comes down to this," Kit said, folding her hands in front of her on the table. She still wore a bandage around her ring finger. "As head of production, you see the issue only in terms of cost to the customer and profit for the company."

Ryan nodded and made himself relax in his chair. Listening to the other side's grievances was his specialty. He'd let her talk it out, and then she'd be more willing to hear his side and to compromise. "Go on."

She unfolded and refolded her hands. "We're supposed to be putting together a compelling proposal for the Winstons. I'm not in sales, but I believe that it takes more than low bids to win loyal customers."

Ryan nodded again and tried for an encouraging expression. A weak ray of winter sunlight broke through the overcast sky and found its way into the room. Kit sat right in its line of fire, and the ray of sun turned her hair into a glowing red-and-gold blaze. He'd never seen anything so beautiful.

"We want the Winstons' business this year, and for many years to come." She paused and raised a hand to her hair. "Is there something wrong? You keep staring at my head."

"No," he said quickly. "It's lovely. I mean—I'm just listening to what you have to say. I think you have some good points, some very good points." What the hell was he talking about? He had to pay attention, but she mesmerized him with her flaming hair, delicate nose and full mouth. Wonderful lips that wanted to be kissed, he could tell.

"So what do you think?" she asked.

He blinked and lifted his gaze from her mouth to her eyes. She'd been talking, and he'd only been able to watch her mouth without paying attention to the words. "What do I think?"

She tapped the pages in front of her. "Yes. Don't you agree that the Winstons' specs are wrong?"

He glanced at the spec sheets. They were identical to the ones he'd been working from. "You're convinced they're wrong," he said to give himself time.

She chewed on her lower lip and picked at the bandage on her ring finger. "Yes, I think the gauge specs are off. Too thin, much too thin."

"Hmm," he murmured. Increasing the gauge of the metal would raise the cost too much. That was a bottom-line issue they couldn't get around.

Kit continued to pick at the tape on her finger. "As I said, they'll save money initially, but lose all their savings in the percentage of unusable containers. These tins will dent while being filled at their factory. And more will be damaged when shipped.''

He reached over and covered her hand with his. ''You're going to pull that tape off any second.''

She gazed at him with wide eyes, but didn't try to move her hand. ''I didn't know I was doing it,'' she said. ''Just nervous, I guess.''

''Why should you be nervous?'' He kept hold of her hand, and she didn't protest.

''You make me nervous. You know that.'' She did that chewing thing with her lower lip again, so he had to look at her mouth once more. That wonderful, kissable mouth.

''I don't intend to,'' he said softly, and moved his chair closer to hers. ''How's your finger holding up?'' He examined the gauze wrapping. It had been more securely anchored than yesterday's, but now was nearly unhinged.

''It's fine.'' She lifted her gaze to meet his, then lowered her lashes.

There was no way he could resist her. He leaned closer and she tipped her head to one side.

''Oh, my gosh'' said a voice from the doorway behind him.

Kit pulled away from him and turned pink.

Ryan rotated in his seat and faced a young woman with curly brown hair, the same one who'd interrupted a similar moment the day before. She was fast becoming a major irritation in his life. ''Cynthia, I believe?'' he said, standing up and extending his right hand. ''I'm Ryan Holt.''

Cynthia stood uncertainly in the doorway. ''Yes, I know. I'm sorry...'' Her gaze fell on his outstretched hand and she hastened forward to shake it. ''I'm Kit's assistant. I didn't know you were in here.'' She looked past Ryan to Kit, her face scrunched into an apologetic grimace while she continued to pump Ryan's arm up and down.

"Pleased to meet you," Ryan said, and looked significantly at their joined hands.

"Oh, gosh," she said, and released his hand in midswing. "Me, too. Sorry I barged in. I'll come back later."

"It's all right, Cynthia." Kit stood up and busied herself straightening the papers on the table. "We were just discussing the Winston proposal."

"That's what I came in for, actually. Mr. Calvert left a message. He didn't want to disturb you, but he hoped the proposal was coming along. Those were his words."

Kit leveled a look at Ryan. "How is the proposal coming along? I gave you my position, but you didn't tell me what you thought."

"You made a convincing argument. It's a quality-control issue. We have to recommend the thicker gauge. But that certainly means you'll have to give ground on the four-color printing."

"That's impossible. Their design calls for full-color."

Ryan shrugged. "Their design called for a thinner gauge, too. Let's propose they go with the two-color, or better yet, one-color, and we can bring in a strong bid."

"You don't understand," she said as if she were explaining her point to a particularly dim-witted person. "They have identified their product with the more elaborate graphic that can only be executed in four-color printing."

He folded his arms across his chest. "I understand very well that they can adapt to a different design if it's in their economic interest."

Kit put her hands on her hips and stuck out her chin.

How had they reached this impasse? A few minutes ago all he could think of was kissing her silly.

"Excuse me?" Cynthia said, sidling in between them. "I think Ryan could be right."

Kit shot Cynthia a look that didn't bode well for her employment future at Calvert. "Thanks for sharing that, Cynthia, but Ryan and I have to work this out together."

"Yes, I know. And I see that you can," Cynthia said, her gaze darting from one of them to the other.

He had to hand it to the kid. She was resilient—or else she didn't know any better. "How?" he asked.

"The two-color design is Kit's forte." She pointed to a plaque on the wall behind Kit's desk. "She won the ASCM Notable Achievement Award her first year here at Calvert. And that was for a two-color design. Right, Kit?"

Ryan raised an eyebrow at Kit, but she wouldn't meet his gaze. "You don't say." He strolled over to the plaque and gazed at it. "I didn't realize that you did the graphic designing yourself. I thought you just executed the ones the clients submit."

"I do both," Kit admitted.

"Then you could do something for the Winstons," he suggested.

"Not by tomorrow morning, I couldn't," she protested.

Cynthia stood in the middle of the office, smiling widely.

Ryan caught Cynthia's eye, and she nodded in the affirmative to him. "I'm not suggesting you do a final design," he said, "but a sketch or two? You could manage that, couldn't you? I'll do all the cost and production time projections."

Kit bowed her head and ran her fingertips across her temples. "All right," she said at last. She raised her head and looked at him. "Do a set of costs for a one-color, as well. I'll work up something that has cutouts to show the metal underneath.'' She turned to Cynthia. "You'll be working late tonight.''

"Great,'' Cynthia said, her enthusiasm undimmed.

"I'll be here, too,'' Ryan said.

"That won't be necessary. You're doing all the costing and time projections. The report format you worked up looks fine to me. Just send over the numbers. Cynthia will incorporate them into the report.'' She turned away from him and crossed to her desk. It was a dismissal, plain and simple.

"So I guess I can tell Mr. Calvert that the proposal is coming along really well, right?'' Cynthia asked him.

"Yes, you do that,'' Ryan said on his way out of the office. He'd won his point. The proposal was in the bag, and he didn't even have to work late. So why did he feel so let down?

Kit clasped the report folders to her chest and led Cynthia into the empty conference room. In a few minutes it would be the moment of truth with the Winstons, and she had butterflies in her stomach at the thought of it. The deep carpet smothered the sound of their footsteps, and the long walnut table gleamed at them, its mirrorlike polish daring them to smudge the surface with their fingerprints.

"I've never been in here before,'' Cynthia said in a near whisper.

Kit glanced at her. If the ever-bubbly Cynthia was daunted by the empty room, how was she going to support Kit when it was filled with their new clients and Calvert executives? She handed the pile of folders to Cynthia. "I'll arrange the chairs, and you put a folder at each place.''

Kit circled the table, pulled three chairs away and re-arranged the remaining chairs to make the space between them even. Cynthia followed after her and set out the folders one by one.

"This report looks so fantastic," Cynthia said with her more typical effervescence. "You'd think we'd spent two weeks on it, instead of two days. Ryan's way of doing things really has made a difference."

"It wasn't Ryan's idea to do it in two days, you know. Mr. and Mrs. Winston set the meeting for today. They're the ones who have the radically different business prac-tices."

"Anyone who calls their company Mom and Popcorn, and makes it work, is already pretty different. We'd never have pulled this off without Ryan, though."

"You and I had something to do with it, too, Cynthia. We were the ones who stayed till ten last night."

"I think Ryan would have stayed if you'd let him. I know you're not married and all that, but why can't you even be in the same room with him?"

That was a question she didn't want to answer, even to herself. "I'll be in the same room today. And I think the whole project ran more efficiently because we avoided endless face-to-face meetings."

"I agree with Kit," Ryan said from the doorway.

"Oh!" Cynthia gave a little squeak and clutched her chest. "I didn't hear you come in."

Kit turned to gaze at him. For an eerie split second she saw him as she'd seen him for the first time at Lindsay's wedding—the dark-haired stranger with the charming smile.

Cynthia crossed to join Ryan by the door. "We were just setting up the room for the meeting. Did you see the final version we left for you last night?"

"Thanks, I saw it, and it looks great." He glanced down at the papers he held in his hand. "You know what?" he said to Cynthia. "I left it on my desk. Would you do me a big favor and get it for me? Kit and I need to go over a few things before the Winstons get here."

"We have another copy of the report for you here," Kit said, pointing to the folders on the table. She needed Cynthia as a buffer. Yesterday had taught her it wasn't a good idea to be alone with him.

"I know, but I made some notes on the copy you left for me," Ryan said.

"I can get it. No problem," Cynthia said, and hurried out the door.

"Thanks, Cynthia," he called after her. He leveled his gaze at Kit. "You look tired. How late did you stay last night?"

Kit shrugged. "Nine or so," she fudged.

"We could have finished it faster together."

"Cynthia helped. I thought it would make it easier all around if we weren't seen together."

He raised his eyebrows. "Easier?"

"You know, gossip." And, not to mention, her getting into a situation to cause gossip, like nearly kissing him with Cynthia looking on.

"Maybe you're right. At any rate, we worked together very well without actually being together. I'll admit that having this thrown at me first thing felt like learning to swim by being thrown off the end of the pier. You were a big help."

She couldn't help grinning at the image. "Like water wings?"

"More like shark repellent."

"No one wants you to fail. Everyone's rooting for your success."

"It's *our* success," he said. "Or it will be, if we pull this off."

"I know, it's that big 'if,'" she said, clutching at her stomach.

"What's the matter? Nerves got you?"

"A little," she admitted.

"Don't let them. You're going to do fine." He smiled at her, and instead of settling down, the butterflies redoubled their flutterings.

Cynthia popped her head into the room. "Ryan? There's an urgent call for you."

"Who is it?" he asked.

Cynthia shrugged. "I don't know. You can take it in Lorraine's office. It's closest."

"Thanks," he said. He turned to Kit, a worry line forming between his eyebrows. "I can't imagine what that is. Tell John I'll be right back, okay?"

She nodded and watched him rush out the door. What could be so important it couldn't wait until after this meeting?

She heard voices in the hallway. Two seconds later, John Calvert ushered in the Winstons. Cynthia followed them into the room. "Here we are," John announced.

Harriet Winston hurried forward, her hand outstretched to Kit. "Hello, I'm Harriet," she said, without waiting for John to make introductions. She gestured with her head toward her husband. "That's Arthur."

"Nice to meet you. I'm Kit." She shook Harriet's hand. She was in her late fifties, a short, compact woman with a round face and a warm smile, and she apparently wasn't interested in formality.

Arthur Winston shook her hand, too. "How do you do, Kit?" He was only a few inches taller than his wife, and if his smile wasn't as wide as hers, it was as warm.

She was going to have a hard time staying nervous around these two, except one part of her kept waiting for Ryan to come back.

"Ryan will be here in just a minute. He received an urgent phone call," Kit explained.

"I hope it's nothing serious," Harriet said.

"Probably not," Kit said with an assurance she didn't feel. He had such a big family. How could you keep so many loved ones safe?

Ryan came in the room and stood by the door. His face told part of the story. Whatever it was, it was very serious.

"Kit? Could I have a word with you?"

"Me?" she said. Why would he be looking at her like that? "What is it? Is it your family?"

He shook his head and, if anything, looked more solemn.

She moved toward him. "What? Tell me, please." That look on his face. It was her family, not his. "Is it Mary?" She couldn't get out more than a whisper. "Please, Ryan, tell me it isn't Mary."

She reached for him, and he opened his arms and drew her to him. "She's in the hospital," he said, his mouth against her hair. "She's going to make it, but Warren needs you. I told him I'd bring you right away."

Chapter Seven

Kit followed Ryan past the automatic doors into the main lobby of Reno Community Hospital. She hesitated and looked around, but Ryan strode directly to the information desk and spoke to a gray-haired volunteer in a pink pinafore. Ryan would take care of finding the way to the Coronary Care Unit, just as he'd taken care of excusing them from the meeting, getting her home and packed, and booking them both on the next flight to Reno. Everything he'd done had taken the nightmare edge off the moment, making it real and manageable, so that now, here they were, finding the way to Mary's room in the most matter-of-fact way.

Ryan returned to her side and took her by the elbow. "It's this way," he said, and guided her down a brightly lit corridor. Arrows posted at every intersection directed them to Coronary Care.

She hadn't been inside a hospital since her mother died, but the feeling of the place was instantly familiar. The overbright fluorescent lights. The brief spates of noise that burst through a blanket of hush. The odors of antiseptic, flowers and human suffering intermingled. She breathed in the air. Yes, that was the smell of grief. She remembered it now.

They reached the double doors marked Coronary Care Unit Waiting Room. Ryan pulled Kit to a stop. "Are you okay?" he asked, bending down a little to peer into her face.

"Sure," she said automatically. "I'm fine."

He frowned as if he didn't believe her.

"I will be fine," she amended. "Just as soon as I know that Mary's going to be all right."

He nodded and took her bandaged left hand. "Good thing you changed your mind about having the ring cut off."

"I didn't have time," she said quickly. Plus, when she thought about Lindsay's reaction, she couldn't bring herself to do it.

"I think you'd better take off the camouflage before you go in there," he said, and pulled at the bandage.

She reached to undo the tape, but Ryan had already loosened it. One tug and the gauze wrapping came off in his hand.

"I don't know about you," he said, tucking the bandage away in his jacket pocket, "but I'm having the strangest sensation of déjà vu."

She glanced up at his face and found him staring at her mouth, and before she could blink once, he bent down, touched his lips to hers in the most fleeting kiss and straightened again.

She touched her mouth with her fingertips. "What was that for?"

"To break the déjà vu curse."

"What curse? I never heard of such a thing."

"It's a terrible jinx. I'd be forever taking that gauze wrapping off your finger, thinking I'd like to kiss you, and never allowed to because your assistant or somebody would walk in on us. And look," he said, indicating the hallway with a wave of his hand, "even in a busy hospital, no one showed up. I broke the curse." He pushed the door open and held it for her to pass through.

She hesitated for a moment on the threshold. She'd been having her own déjà vu experience. It hadn't had anything to do with wanting to kiss Ryan, but his kissing her had banished it anyway, at least temporarily.

She walked into the waiting room and found Warren slumped in an ugly orange plastic chair, staring at a blank television screen. His silver hair stuck out at every angle, his collar lay half in, half out of his jacket.

"Warren?"

He straightened and looked up. "Kit. Ryan." His gaze darted from her face to Ryan's and back again. "Thank God, you're here," he said, rising to his feet to embrace her. He held on to her for a good half minute, as if she were a lifeline in a sea of impending loss. She closed her eyes to stop their burning. She'd be strong for Warren, if that was what he needed. Goodness knew, he'd been strong for her in the bad times.

Warren drew back, but still held Kit by the shoulders. "I couldn't reach Lindsay. I left a message. That's all I could do."

"Lindsay's out of town. I'm sorry, but I don't have a number for her." She took him by the arm, led him back to the chairs and sat down with him. Ryan settled into a seat next to her.

"Maybe it's best," Warren said. "Sometimes Lindsay can get very emotional around these kinds of situations."

"Do you have any news about Mary?" Ryan asked.

"They have to put in a pacemaker. The doctor said there was every reason to think she'll be fine." He ran his hand through his hair. "We were going to leave today. We came to Reno instead because she wasn't feeling well. Came right into the emergency room, and she..." He stopped and covered his eyes with one hand.

Kit took his other hand and squeezed it. "Ryan told me. She collapsed, and they had to resuscitate her. So lucky that you came directly here. You were in the right place."

Warren dropped his hand from his eyes and looked at her. "You're right. It was both so unfortunate and so fortunate all at once. I didn't know how serious her condition was. She kept it from me. She should have had a pacemaker put in before this, but she resisted. I don't know why."

Kit reached over and straightened his collar. "Have you seen her?"

"Yes. She's sedated and drowsy, but I know she'll want to see you. I'll tell them you're here. We have to communicate with the nurses' station by phone." He got up and crossed to the phone.

Kit stood up, too. She wasn't ready to see Mary. "Wait. There's no need to disturb her if she's resting."

He waved her off. "She asked for you. I told her I'd send you in as soon as you got here." He picked up the phone and murmured into the mouthpiece.

Ryan put his hand on her shoulder, and she turned to face him. "Don't worry about Warren," he said. "I'll take him to the cafeteria and get him to eat something. He'll be okay. You go on in."

Kit looked back at Warren. He moved toward the door to the unit, motioning her to join him. There was nothing for it. She had to go in, but her feet remained glued to the floor. What was wrong with her? Mary wanted to see her. And she'd like nothing more than to see Mary—but her Mary, not the frail and wan Mary tied to monitors and IV lines who lay on the other side of the waiting room door.

Ryan wrapped an arm around her shoulders and gave her a gentle shake. "Everything is going to be okay. I'll take good care of Warren. You visit with Mary for as long as they'll let you."

She glanced at him and then away. He'd be shocked if he knew how much she dreaded seeing Mary. A nurse stood in the doorway, holding the door open for the next visitor. Her feet carried her away from Ryan, and past Warren to the nurse who waited to escort her into the unit.

"You're Mrs. Franklin's daughter?" the nurse asked.

For a second Kit hesitated. If she said no, would they stop her from coming in? She smiled at the nurse and said, "I'm Kit. How is she?" and kept walking forward.

"She's stable right now," the nurse said. "Did you have a chance to talk to the doctor?"

Kit shook her head. The nurse led her past cubicles curtained on three sides. Kit kept her eyes forward until the nurse made a sharp right, entered one of the cubicles and paused at Mary's bedside. Kit hovered at the foot of the bed. Mary lay motionless, with her eyes closed. Kit couldn't even see her chest move as she breathed.

"Mrs. Franklin?" the nurse said. "Your daughter's here to see you."

Mary's eyes opened instantly and searched for a moment before her gaze landed on Kit. She smiled so sweetly then, Kit's heart tightened in her chest. "Kit, dear, you came."

"Of course I came. What else would I do?"

The nurse moved away from the side of the bed and made room for Kit to slip in next to Mary. "You can stay ten minutes," the nurse advised her.

Mary lifted her hand. Kit reached over the bed rails and took it in her own. Mary's hand was icy cold.

"Are you warm enough?" Kit asked, testing Mary's arm with her other hand.

"I hardly know what I am," Mary answered. "I'm as doped up as a shanghaied sailor. If I drift off, just give me a little nudge, will you?" The words were pure Mary, but her voice was a faded version of the original.

"Why would I do that? You're supposed to be resting."

"Tell *them* that. Every time I do go to sleep, someone comes in and takes my blood pressure or pokes me with a needle."

"I'm sorry," Kit said. "Do you want me to say something to the doctor?"

Mary squeezed her hand and smiled gently. "No, of course not. I'm the one who should be sorry. Poor Warren, he's so upset. I hope he'll forgive me."

"What's to forgive?" Kit said. "You couldn't help getting sick. It wasn't your fault."

"It was, though. I knew it was just a matter of time. My doctor warned me it could be dangerous for me not to have the pacemaker, but I wanted to wait."

"Why? Are you afraid of the surgery?"

Mary paused and looked away from Kit for a few moments. "Yes, I suppose I was afraid, but not the way you think. I was afraid for you."

"For me?"

"Yes, there are complications sometimes. And I was afraid of what would happen to you if—if I died."

Kit hung on to Mary's hand. As frail as it was, it was

her security. Mary had said the one thing Kit had barely allowed herself even to think. But Mary couldn't die. She just couldn't. "Mary, please…" Kit couldn't go on.

"It's all right. I'm not afraid now, because you have Ryan."

"Ryan?"

"Yes, he's your perfect mate. I knew you'd find him eventually. But I worried that if anything happened to me, you might close yourself off completely, the way you did after your mother died. Now I know everything's going to be just fine."

Ryan pushed his empty bowl to one side and watched Warren trying to be a good sport about eating his own soup. He could take his time. The cafeteria wasn't too busy at this hour. They could hang out here for a while longer.

Warren put his spoon down and glanced apologetically at Ryan. "I'm afraid I can't finish my soup, even though it's really quite tasty. Surprising, isn't it? You generally think of hospital food as indigestible."

"How about some coffee?" Ryan asked.

"That sounds like a good idea." Ryan moved to stand, but Warren waved him off. "Allow me to do the honors." He headed off in the direction of the hot tables.

Ryan settled down into his chair again. Getting Warren to come into the cafeteria had been a good idea. He already looked a little more like his usual self. He'd seemed to welcome the chance to talk, telling and retelling the story of Mary's collapse.

Best for Warren to describe it to him, anyway. Kit hadn't looked as if she could handle the grim details very well. From that first bad moment when she'd guessed that something had happened to Mary, she'd looked like someone living a nightmare.

He checked his watch. Hard to believe it was only two in the afternoon. The Winstons were long gone from the meeting at Calvert—if they had even stayed for the meeting after he and Kit had run out on them. Maybe he should call and see if anything had come of the meeting, or if the Winstons had decided Calvert's personnel were too unreliable. At the very least he should find out if he still had a job there.

Warren came back to the table with two cups of coffee. "I forgot to ask you if you take cream or sugar."

"Black is fine," Ryan said.

Warren lowered himself into his chair and fiddled with the handle of his coffee cup. Finally he cleared his throat and said, "Mary and I are extremely happy about your marriage to Kit. I hope you know that."

Ryan shifted his feet under the table. Warren was such a decent guy. It was wrong to go on lying to him about the marriage. Now that the worst had happened, what difference would it make if he and Mary knew the truth? But he couldn't make the unilateral decision to tell Warren, and Kit would undoubtedly say no. He cleared his throat in turn. "Thanks, I appreciate your telling me."

"You know that we regard Kit as our daughter," Warren said.

"I see how close you are. I know she's devoted to both of you."

"Did she tell you that we wanted to adopt her legally?"

Ryan straightened in his chair. What Kit hadn't told him in the course of their nonmarriage would fill an encyclopedia, but this was a particularly interesting item. "No, she hasn't mentioned it."

Warren sighed. "She wouldn't agree to it. She said she didn't want to have to depend on us." He shook his head. "She was only thirteen."

"Sounds like Kit, all right."

"She worked in the summer during high school and college. I guess you know about her Stanford scholarship."

Ryan made a noncommittal sound.

"What I'm leading up to is that she would never take anything from us. Nothing material, that is. Room and board, that was it. But Mary and I decided to make both Lindsay and Kit our legal heirs. Lindsay knows and is in agreement. Everything will be divided between the two of them."

"And Kit doesn't know?"

Warren shook his head. "We thought it best not to tell her. But after this scare with Mary, I thought maybe, if you knew…" Warren left the sentence unfinished.

"If I knew?" he prompted.

"You'd make her accept her inheritance."

Ryan took a sip of coffee. He'd walked into quicksand the day he'd agreed to go along with this phony marriage. How could he have been so stupid? "All this is pretty hypothetical, isn't it? I mean, I know Mary's health isn't so great right now, but you look fit."

"You're right. The doctor tells me I'll live to be a hundred, though I can't think why I'd want to if I didn't have Mary. But that's neither here nor there. The point is that Mary has her own money. On her passing, it will go into trust funds for Lindsay and Kit and pay out a very handsome sum annually. It would be a comfort to both of us to know that Kit wouldn't object to the terms of the will."

How was he going to get out of this? "I have to be honest with you, Warren. I'm not…"

Warren looked at him expectantly.

"I have very little influence with Kit."

"I can't believe that."

"Believe it."

"But you convinced her to marry you."

Ryan leaned forward in his chair. "I'll let you in on a little secret. It was all Kit's idea."

Warren stared at him, his eyes wide in amazement. "Really?"

Ryan nodded and leaned back in his chair. He'd found a way out of the quicksand at last.

"Mary was right, after all," Warren said, almost to himself.

"Pardon?"

Warren beamed at him. "Mary said you were Kit's perfect mate, just as Kit is yours. She's always thought Kit would change her ideas about marriage when she found the right man. I must admit I thought it a bit of romanticizing on her part, but you've proved me wrong."

"I wouldn't go that far," Ryan protested.

"I would," Warren said with more energy than he'd shown all day. "I'd say that Kit's falling in love with you has changed her completely. I withdraw my request. You don't need to convince her, I'm sure that with you at her side she'll see Mary's bequest in the right light."

Ryan stared at Warren. How could he have been so deluded as to think he was out of the quicksand? The suffocating stuff was even now slowly closing over the top of his head.

The orange chairs in the waiting room didn't grow any more comfortable or any less ugly as the day inched along. Several times Kit found herself staring at the blank television screen just as she'd seen Warren doing earlier. Later, when members of other families crowded into the room, waiting in turn for their brief bedside visits, someone turned the television on, and she watched a program along with everyone else. When it was over, she couldn't for the life of her remember what it had been about.

Ryan and Warren sat with her, Warren in turns solicitous about her and worried about Mary. Ryan made sure she had food and drink, anything she wanted, and a few things she didn't want but ate anyway, just to keep him from hovering over her. Not that he hovered, exactly. He watched—his gaze meeting hers again and again whenever she glanced in his direction. Even while he encouraged Warren to talk and distracted him with conversation, he watched her. What did he want from her?

He brought her a turkey sandwich and a cup of coffee that Warren insisted she have. She rejected the coffee and sent him back for tea, just to get a respite from him. Didn't he blame her for entangling him in her troubles? What if he lost his job for walking out on the meeting with the Winstons?

If he did lose his job, it would be her fault. All her fault. When he'd told her about Mary, she'd headed straight into his arms. He'd taken over from there, and she'd let him. And because she'd let him take over, he was here, playing the role of her husband again.

Although, she couldn't tell by looking that he was acting a part. He'd bent his head toward Warren and asked would it be all right if he made hotel reservations for them? Warren thought a suite would be a good idea and smiled his approval at her, because Ryan arranged the whole thing in a minute without any fuss at all. How would she ever convince Mary and Warren that they wanted to get a divorce?

Her perfect mate, Mary had said. She should tell Mary the truth.

When afternoon faded into evening, Ryan buttonholed Mary's doctor and brought him into the waiting room. The doctor was still dressed in scrubs, from having been in surgery all day saving the lives of other patients. His surgical mask hung around his neck, and tufts of curly gray hair stuck out from under his green cotton cap. He looked tired, but he seemed happy enough to talk to them about Mary.

Kit twisted her fingers together while the doctor's words washed over her, the exact phrases escaping her, but their essential significance remaining. If everything went as planned, if there were no complications, Mary would be all right. Ryan made the doctor repeat his words and looked hard at Kit as if he wanted to make sure she'd heard.

She gazed at Ryan while she thanked the doctor. She should have told Mary the truth. It wasn't too late, she could still confess.

She sat down in one of the ugly orange chairs and didn't say anything.

Chapter Eight

Ryan held the door of their hotel suite open for Kit, and Warren stepped back to let her precede him. She crossed into a large and elegant living room with enough sofas and chairs to accommodate twelve comfortably. Two doors, one at each end of the room, must lead to the bedrooms.

"Which room is ours?" Kit asked Ryan.

Ryan pointed to the door on the right. "Our bags are already in there. I had them brought up earlier."

She crossed to the door he indicated, opened it and stepped into a bedroom with two beds. Well, what had she expected? Of course Ryan had arranged to have a room with two beds. They weren't actually married. They weren't anything to each other. That wasn't quite true. Ryan meant something to her—something she could barely let herself think about.

Through the sheer curtains on the window the city lights blinked and glittered. Warren's and Ryan's deep voices came to her as a murmur from the other room.

Warren had turned to Ryan more and more during the day for help with practical details as well as for moral support. She owed it to Ryan to come clean with Warren and Mary about their relationship. She should have done it earlier in the day, when he still had time to fly back to San Francisco. And yet, when she'd had the chance to say something, she hadn't taken it.

She turned away from the window. Selfishness, that was what it amounted to, pure selfishness, because nothing in her life had felt so right to her as the moment that morning when she'd walked into the shelter of his arms. Mary's life was threatened, and yet somehow Ryan had made her feel as if everything was going to be okay, simply because he was there with her.

But those were her feelings, not his. He'd taken care of her, but she hadn't given him a choice. She should do the right thing and tell Warren the truth. She should, but she hadn't, and she wasn't going to. She'd wait for him to say it was time for a "divorce." And that would be another lie.

She twisted the ring on her left hand. When had she become so dishonest? She gave the ring a tug and it slid off her finger. She stared at the ornate gold circle. Why did it come off now, when before it wouldn't even budge? She closed her fist over the ring. She knew an omen when she saw one. She was supposed to tell the truth.

She strode back into the living room. Ryan and Warren broke off their conversation and looked at her expectantly. Okay, she was ready, but how did she begin? "Would you like some tea, Warren?" she asked. Was her brain being controlled by aliens? What did tea have to do with telling the truth? She just had to say it—*I'm not married to Ryan.* "I—I could call down for some, if you'd like."

"No, thank you, my dear. In fact, I was just telling Ryan that I'm going to turn in."

"So soon? It's early yet," she said.

"It's been a very long day for me," Warren said. He had a slump to his shoulders she'd never seen before.

"Of course," she said, crossing immediately to his side. "I wasn't thinking. Get some rest." She kissed him on the cheek. She'd simply have to wait until tomorrow to tell him. Maybe there'd be time to rehearse her speech before then.

Warren smiled and patted her on the shoulder. "Take care of her, Ryan," he said.

Ryan came up and put his arm around Kit's waist. "You know I will. We'll all get a good night's sleep and be ready to see Mary before they take her in for surgery in the morning."

Kit could feel the warmth of Ryan's hand where it rested at her waist. They must look the very image of a happily married couple—an illustration labeled What's Wrong With This Picture? She clenched her fist around the ring and felt its hard edges against the flesh of her hand.

Warren crossed into his own bedroom and closed the door behind him.

"You mentioned tea," Ryan said, dropping his arm and stepping away from her. "Would you like some?"

"No," she said quickly, and turned away. She liked being close to him. She liked it too much for her own good.

"Are you sure?"

"Of course I'm sure. I hope I know my own mind."

"What's the matter?"

"Nothing." What was wrong with her? She'd decided to be honest, now was her chance to let him know her intentions. Then she wouldn't be able to get out of telling Warren tomorrow. "Wait a minute," she said, turning to face him and holding out her hand, palm up. "I wanted to show you this." Lindsay's ring glinted in the lamplight.

He picked up the ring, looked at it, then raised his gaze to meet hers. "When did you get it off?"

"Just now. I don't know why it came off so easily."

"You probably lost weight skipping meals while you were working on the Winston presentation."

How did he know she'd missed meals during the last few days?

He gave the ring back to her. "Better put it on. You might not be able to tomorrow."

"No, I want to tell Warren and Mary the truth."

"You want to tell them now? It's a good thing you're not a comedian, because your timing is terrible."

"I thought you'd be glad. Don't you want to have everything out in the open?"

"We've gone too far for that."

"We have?" She didn't get it. He was the one who'd been pushing her to tell the truth right from the beginning.

"Most definitely." He placed himself squarely in front of her. So close she could easily have slipped her arms around him and rested her forehead against his shoulder. Or fit the palm of her hand to the curve of his jaw and reached up and kissed him. She could have, but she didn't. Instead, she dropped her gaze and stared at the ring she still held in her hand and watched her hand tremble slightly, because she knew what she wanted now. She wanted Ryan.

"Let me see that ring again," he said. He took her left hand in his and slipped the ring halfway onto her finger. "It's still a little tight, isn't it?"

She didn't answer. She couldn't. His touch, always so gentle, turned her insides into melted marshmallow.

"Tell you what," he said, removing the ring from her finger.

She lifted her gaze to meet his. His eyes were dark, but were they black or very dark brown? Even as close as she was to him right now, she couldn't tell.

"I'll just…" He stopped midsentence.

His eyes seemed to grow even darker. Was that possible? She leaned a little closer to see.

"Kit?"

"Mmm?"

"I think I'm going to kiss you."

"Oh, good," she said on a sigh, and tilted her head to meet his mouth with hers. She'd kissed him before and knew about the movement of his mouth against hers, and how it made her want to press her entire body close to his. Even so, this kiss was brand-new, like some wonderful present she wanted to unwrap slowly and savor.

She slid her hands upward. She simply had to caress his chin and feel the rough stubble of his beard against her fingers. But he did something very interesting to her lower lip, and she forgot what she was about and slipped her hands inside his jacket, flattening them against his chest instead. Through the material of his shirt she could feel the heat of his skin and the beating of his heart. Those sensations alone were enough to raise her own pulse and spread warmth over her skin, although that might have happened, anyway, because he pulled her close against his body, his hands hot and firm against the small of her back.

She had to be closer still, so she wrapped her arms around his neck and pressed herself full-length against him. He made a sort of growling sound in his throat, and she laughed, tilting her head back and letting the sound bubble out of her.

"What's so funny?" he asked, and pressed his mouth to her neck.

"Nothing. Everything," she said, tilting her head to one side as he nibbled up her throat to her ear.

He lifted his head and smiled at her. "Did I ever tell you how your kisses affect me?"

She laughed again. "The topic hasn't come up. I can't imagine why."

"Your kisses short-circuit my brain. Even the first time, when you blindsided me. I was mad that you'd run in front of my car. Then all of that disappeared, and there was just you and me, kissing."

He'd got it exactly right. The rest of the world had simply fallen away. "So you were about to say something just now, but you kissed me instead, and now you've forgotten what it was?"

"You've got it," he said, and kissed the tip of her nose. "Wait a second. I remember now—the ring." He relaxed his embrace and held up Lindsay's ring. "I was thinking, why don't I go out and buy you a ring that fits?"

"Now? Tonight?"

"Sure. This is Reno, remember? What kind would you like? Something like this?"

"No," she said, and paused. He was talking about buying her a wedding ring. Did he want to go on pretending? Or could he mean something more serious?

"I agree." He gave a judicious nod. "This ring isn't

you at all. You want something simple, right? Something elegant in its simplicity."

That was exactly what she'd like. He knew her taste so well, it was uncanny. "Yes, I'd prefer something simple, but why bother? It's only for tomorrow, isn't it? And then I can take it off for good."

He hesitated a moment. "Not quite. The Winstons think that we're married. They've invited us to their country house so we can finish our presentation."

"The Winstons?"

"Yes. That's why it's handy that we actually like each other," he said, and dropped another kiss on her mouth. "Because as far as the rest of the world is concerned, we're married."

Kit froze. What could he mean "handy that they liked each other"? She'd been thinking about kisses that made the world fall away and about belonging to someone, not about how convenient it was that they didn't find each other repulsive.

"What's the matter?" he asked, peering into her face.

Her throat seemed to have closed up, and she had to clear it before she could speak. "Would you mind going over that again? The part about the Winstons."

"I called the office, and surprisingly enough, the Winstons liked the drama of the situation. They were particularly happy to hear that we were married. John Calvert seems to think that there's an excellent chance that we'll get the contract if we go to their house and make our presentation."

"So John thinks we're married, too?"

"Not anymore. I told him the whole story, and his reaction was that we had to go for it as a married couple, because that's what the Winstons want to hear. So what do you think?'' he said, holding up the ring. ''Shall we get a ring that fits?''

She snatched it out of his hand and jammed it on her finger. ''There's no need. This ring is 'handy,' and it fits well enough.'' She couldn't believe she'd been so stupid. Ryan wasn't interested in a serious relationship with her. She was simply convenient.

''What's wrong?'' he asked, taking her hand.

She pulled away from his grasp. ''Nothing. I'm tired, that's all.''

He folded his arms. ''It bothers you about the Winstons. That's it, isn't it? Pretending that we're married.''

''Yes,'' she said, grabbing at any explanation. ''I told you. I don't want to be married, even if it's only pretend. I thought you felt the same way.''

''You know I hate lying. But it's complicated now. John expects us to secure the Winston contract. You probably have pretty good job security, but John made it clear that my job is on the line here. I helped you fool Warren and Mary. It's only fair that you help me with the Winstons.''

She ducked her head. He was right. She owed him for everything he'd done for her. And she couldn't hold it against him that she'd come to want more from him. That was her fault.

She lifted her head and arranged a smile on her face. ''You're right. I'll do anything I can to help.'' She forced a yawn. ''Excuse me,'' she said, patting her mouth. ''I'm pretty tired. I think I'll get some sleep.'' She moved away from him before he could act on any impulse to kiss her good-night.

''Sure,'' he said. ''Good night.''

She crossed to the bedroom door, opened it, then looked back at Ryan for a moment. His brow was creased in a frown, but he made no move to follow her. "Good night," she said.

She stepped into the bedroom and closed the door behind her, keeping her hand on the doorknob for a few seconds. She could turn around, march back in there and throw herself into his arms. But what good would that do? Ryan thought it was "handy" that they liked each other. That put their relationship right up there with an electric drill and a set of socket wrenches. She let go of the door handle and moved away from the door.

Ryan checked his watch and pointed the remote control at the television for another quick run through the channels. There wasn't anything even slightly interesting on at this hour, but somehow he couldn't stop trying to find something. A fit of yawns overtook him, and he let his head sink back on the sofa. Kit should be asleep by now, but just in case she wasn't, he'd give her a few more minutes.

His eyelids drifted shut and an image of Kit, her head tilted just so, ready for kissing, floated before him. He opened his eyes with a jerk. She was so desirable—and so incomprehensible. Scientists would discover what made the dinosaurs extinct long before they figured out why women acted the way they did.

Why did she kiss him one minute like she meant to continue kissing him through the night, and the next minute pull away? He rubbed the back of his neck. The Winston deal was a factor. She didn't want to go on pretending to be married to him. But even without the Winstons, they were stuck with the phony marriage. As soon as he'd taken off with her today, everyone at Calvert was convinced they had a pretty definite relationship.

He wouldn't mind having a real relationship with Kit,

either. Not marriage, of course—he didn't want marriage any more than she did—but something more than a roll between the sheets. Not that he hadn't been having a few fantasies along those lines even before she'd invited his kisses this evening. God, she'd felt so perfect in his arms, her lips so soft and tempting. And that sexy laugh of hers...

He gave his head a shake. He had to get a grip. With her, it was a sexy laugh one minute and a cool good-night the next. Any woman who sent out such mixed messages was trouble.

She understood his work, though. Even with the tension and wrangling between them, they'd come up with a damn good proposal. So, they'd continue to work together. No problem with that, as far as he was concerned. And if he had fantasies about her, that's all they'd be—fantasies. Because he didn't need the irritation of being led on and stopped cold all the time.

He pushed the power button on the remote and let the television blink off. Kit had had more than enough time to fall asleep, and he couldn't keep his eyes open any longer. He turned off the lamps and felt his way to the bedroom door.

As soon as he pushed the door open, he saw her standing by the window. She hadn't drawn the curtains and the city lights cast a faint illumination into the darkened room. What was she doing still awake? She'd better not be waiting up for him. He wasn't in the mood for more of her on-again, off-again routine.

"Kit?" He didn't try to keep his voice soft. "I thought you'd be asleep by now."

She gave a little start and turned her head slightly in his direction. "I was just looking at the lights. I guess I

lost track of time.'' Her voice had a muffled and watery
sound as if she'd been crying.

Great, now what was he going to do? He couldn't just
ignore it and go to bed, could he? He crossed to her side.
''Are you all right?''

''I'm fine,'' she said.

He reached out and touched her cheek. She jerked her
head away, but not before he'd felt the tears. ''What's
the matter? Why are you crying?''

She rubbed her hands over her cheeks. ''It's nothing,
really.''

''Looks like something to me.''

''It's not. Please ignore me. I'm so embarrassed. I
never cry.''

That did it. Why couldn't she wail or sob or clutch at
his shirt and get it wet with her tears? He could deal with
that. He put an arm around her shoulders. She stiffened
at his touch, then shivered.

''You're cold,'' he said. ''Come over here.'' He
steered her toward the bed. ''And tell your hubby all
about it.''

She stopped dead before they reached the bed. ''I don't
want to—'' she hesitated ''—you know...''

''Don't worry. I don't have any dishonorable intentions.'' He pulled back the bed covers.

''I'm still dressed,'' she protested.

And a good thing, too, because she was desirable
enough with clothes on. Not that he was going to try to
go that route with her. He'd just had an example of how
that wouldn't work. ''The clothes don't matter. We just
want to get you warmed up. But you can take off your
shoes.''

She took off her shoes like an obedient child. He piled
up the pillows at the head of the bed and slipped out of

his own shoes. "Okay, get in," he said, holding the covers up for her.

She slid into the bed, moving to one side to leave room for him. He climbed in after her, propped his back against the pillows and gathered her into his arms. She held herself rigid for a moment, then, with a sigh, snuggled her head against his chest.

"Okay, want to tell me what's made you so sad?" he asked.

"Not really. I don't think it would help to talk about it."

He could feel the warmth of her breath through his shirt when she spoke. "I disagree. It always helps to talk things through. Let me guess—it has something to do with Mary."

"Mmm," she murmured.

He'd take that as a yes. Maybe he'd just jump in with both feet. "Why didn't you let Warren and Mary adopt you after your mother died?"

She seemed to stop breathing for a minute, she held so still in his arms. Then, at last, she said, "I guess you and Warren talked a lot today."

It was a statement, not a question. He'd wait and see what else she'd volunteer. It took a full minute before she said, "I told everyone that I wanted to be independent, which was part of it. After my mother died, I just didn't want to belong to anyone again."

"What does that mean, to belong to someone? You mean like family?"

"It means that wherever you go, whatever you do, the person you belong to has a claim on your heart. When they die, or go away, or don't want you anymore, then you're alone. It seemed safer to be alone."

He adjusted his chin to fit on top of her head. The feel

and scent of her hair next to his face had a seductive quality all its own. "It looks like it didn't work," he said.

"What do you mean?"

"You act in every way as if Mary and Warren do have a claim on you."

"I know. It kind of happened when I wasn't looking. Do you know what I mean?"

"Not really," he said, and held himself still while she shifted her body against his to get in a more comfortable position. He had honorable intentions. He really did. He just had to keep reminding all his body parts of that fact.

"When I told them I didn't want to be adopted, they never tried to talk me out of it, but they always acted as if I was their daughter. The next thing I knew, I belonged to them."

"Maybe you should tell them that."

She tilted her head back. "You think I should say it?" she asked.

In the faint light from the window he could just make out the curve of her face. He'd like to get to know that curve first with his hands and then with his lips. "Yes," he said. "I think they need to hear it."

She lowered her cheek to his chest again. He breathed in and out slowly, and his intentions were honorable again, for the moment.

"Thanks, Ryan, for everything."

"You're welcome."

"I mean it. You've been so wonderful. You took care of everything today. I couldn't seem to cope. That's never happened to me before."

Yeah, he was Ryan the Wonderful, just lying here in the dark, thinking maybe she'd be more comfortable without her clothes on. He knew *he* would. "Don't mention it," he mumbled.

"I want you to know that I'll help with the Winston contract. Did you say we're supposed to go to their house?"

"Their country home in Napa. I'm not sure where that is."

"The wine country. An easy drive from the city." She yawned and snuggled closer.

Was she falling asleep? "Kit?" he asked.

"Yes?" she said, her voice low and groggy.

"Out of curiosity, I was wondering, does this belonging thing go the other way, too? Do you have a claim on the other person?"

"Only if they belong to you."

"You know what, Kit?"

"Mmm?"

"You have some very funny ideas."

She didn't answer. Her breathing came soft and even. She must have fallen asleep. It didn't matter. In a few minutes, he'd get up and crawl into the other bed. Right now he'd hold her and take in the scent of her hair. He could relax. He'd kept his word. Of course, the promise held only for tonight. Next time they were in bed together, he wasn't going to be so high-minded. She'd given him an insight that he couldn't let pass by. All he had to do was act as if she belonged to him, and soon enough she'd believe she did. This pretend marriage had hidden benefits.

Kit held Mary's hand and gazed into her smiling face. It was the same scene exactly as yesterday—Mary's bedside in the coronary care unit—but different now in one essential way. Mary's cheeks glowed pink, her hand was warm and her grip firm.

"Mary," Kit said, "you look terrific. I can't believe the difference."

"If I look so terrific, why am I still in the hospital?" Mary asked, the familiar twinkle back in her eye.

"I think it has something to do with the fact that you got out of surgery four hours ago."

"Pooh. You call that surgery? That was nothing compared to when I had my appendix out. Come on, get my clothes for me. I want to go home."

Kit grinned. "The doctor warned me that you were a bit of a handful. Maybe we'll ask that nice nurse to slip something into your IV."

"Please, not that. I'll be good." Mary clasped Kit's hand. "Warren said that your Ryan has been an absolute pillar of support."

"Ryan has been wonderful in every way. I don't know what Warren and I would have done without him."

"I can see how much you love him," Mary said.

Kit stared at her for a moment. "You can?"

"Of course," Mary said. "It shows in your face when you talk about him."

She opened her mouth to protest. She hadn't minded Mary thinking she was in love with Ryan when she wasn't. But now that she knew she had feelings for him, she wanted to deny it. She'd turned into a walking contradiction. And after last night, with Ryan holding her so sweetly in his arms all night long, her feelings for him were stronger than ever. Not feelings of love, of course. Just—feelings. After all, it wasn't as if she belonged to him or anything.

Mary drew her brows together in a worried look. "Kit? Are you all right?"

Kit blinked her eyes to focus them. "I'm fine," she

said automatically. She didn't belong to Ryan, but she did belong to Warren and Mary. "Mary?"

"Yes?"

"Um..." This was harder than she'd thought it would be. "There's something I need to tell you."

"What is it, Kit?"

She took a deep breath. "You know how I've always said that you were like a mother to me? That wasn't quite true. You're not like a mother. You *are* my mother, and Warren's my father. And I'm so glad I belong to both of you."

Mary's eyes filled with tears. "Oh, my dear, thank you," she said, and held up her arms.

"I'm the one who should be doing the thanking," Kit said. She bent over the bed and embraced Mary gently, minding the trailing IV lines. When she straightened up, she saw the nurse standing at the foot of the bed.

"I'm sorry, Mrs. Franklin," the nurse said, "but your daughter's visiting time is up."

Mary gave Kit a special smile. "That's all right. My *daughter* will come back for the next allotted time."

Kit gave Mary's hand one last squeeze and sidled out of the narrow space next to the bed. She retraced her steps to the waiting room. As soon as she pushed the door open, she saw Ryan and Warren seated in the familiar orange chairs.

Ryan stood up and crossed the room to meet her. "How does she look? As good as Warren said?"

She smiled at Warren, who watched them with a fond expression.

"She told me she's ready to go home," she said.

"That's great news," Ryan said, and held out his arms.

She walked into his embrace. It was as natural as breathing to wrap her arms around his middle and tilt her

head back for a kiss. Although, the moment his lips
touched hers, breathing stopped being natural, and she
had to remind herself to inhale. What was that line she'd
been feeding herself—that she had "feelings" for him?
There was no getting around it. She was in love with
him. What was she going to do now?

Chapter Nine

Arthur and Harriet Winston's Napa Valley house came close to what Kit had imagined it would be, stately architecture in the middle of a vineyard. If their house was so predictable, maybe the Winstons themselves wouldn't turn out to be the mavericks they were touted to be. That would be a gift, because her nerves were on edge from trying to imagine what this weekend was going to be like.

Ryan mounted the front steps behind her, carrying their overnight bags. "Some spread," he said. "I wonder if they make their own wine."

"Probably. If they're anything at all like their reputation, they might even stomp their own grapes," she said, and pressed the doorbell.

He put the bags down at his feet. "Now, that's an image." He slanted her a smile.

She turned away and stared at the ornately carved front door. She was far too susceptible to his smiles—and every other kind of expression that flitted across his face. Ever since Mary's surgery, he'd been so solicitous to her, so casually affectionate that she'd had to hold herself in constant check against revealing her feelings for him.

She smoothed the travel wrinkles out of her skirt with the palms of her hands and tugged at the hem of her jacket. "Does the suit look okay? Is it too much like work clothes?"

"The suit's fine. I like the color with your hair."

"Forest green is sort of a cliché on a redhead." Why had she said that? She was so jumpy, she couldn't even take a simple compliment from him. She hurriedly pushed the doorbell again. "Are you sure we have the right weekend? They don't seem to be answering the door."

Ryan reached up and pulled her hand away from the doorbell button. Still holding her hand, he said, "It's a big house. They'll answer eventually. And, getting back to how you look, believe me, nothing could be a cliché on you." He didn't say it lightly, but with a seriousness layered with meaning.

She looked down at their joined hands and up at his face. Once she met his gaze, she couldn't look away. How was she going to make it through the weekend playing this double game of pretending to the Winstons that she loved him while pretending to him that she didn't, when really she did? It was enough to make her head spin. No, her head was spinning because he was holding her hand and moving his thumb back and forth across her knuckles.

She simply had to manage this role, because he didn't love her. He liked her, and she was convenient—that was all.

The door opened, and she almost jerked away from him. Wait, they were supposed to be together. Was she ever going to get this right?

"Hello, so glad you could make it. I'm sorry it took me an age to answer the door," Harriet Winston said, beaming at them both. "Arthur and I were at the other end of the house. I think I could use some roller skates to get around this barn." She ushered them into a most unbarnlike, marble-floored front hall.

Arthur Winston joined them and shook hands with them both. He was only a few inches taller than his short wife, but carried himself with the manner of a much taller man. "That's all we need, Harriet, as soon as our investors get word that you're cruising around the house on roller skates, they'll run for cover."

"We're not investors, Mrs. Winston, but might I suggest a skateboard? You don't have to lace it on," Ryan said.

Harriet Winston whooped with glee at his suggestion, and Arthur chortled. "You're no help," he said, clapping Ryan on the back. "You shouldn't encourage her. She's likely to try it."

Kit smiled along with the others. She'd been worried about how they'd get along with the Winstons, but it had taken Ryan only a minute to charm them both.

"Come this way. Leave your bags there for now. We'll all be more comfortable in the living room. You're not hungry, I hope? We're going to have an early dinner. Is that all right? Arthur and I usually eat early when we're in the country. I don't know why." Harriet chattered them into a spacious room with picture windows overlooking the vineyard.

Harriet and Arthur took two wing chairs, which had the look of being their familiar places. Kit sank into a soft leather sofa, and Ryan joined her. She almost shifted to make room for him but remembered in time to hold still. Ryan settled in next to her so that their bodies touched on one side from hip to knee. How was she supposed to conduct rational conversation under these conditions? She could function when he wasn't touching her, but when he was—well, forget it.

"I was so glad to hear that your mother is better now, Kit," Harriet said.

"Actually, she's so much better, she's even talking about taking on fund-raising for yet another charity."

"I'm sure that having you and Ryan at her side helped her," Arthur said.

It had been a help then, but having Ryan literally at her side right now was making her a nervous wreck.

"We were very sorry that we had to leave so abruptly," Ryan said. "And we appreciate your giving us another shot at presenting our proposal."

Harriet and Arthur exchanged a glance. "Well," Harriet said, scooting forward in her chair. "I'll tell you the truth. We got interested, because no one seemed to know for sure what was going on. As soon as you left, someone said that you were married. Then another said, no, you weren't." She paused and blinked her bright eyes at them.

"We weren't quite as candid about that matter as we might have been," Ryan said.

Harriet and Arthur kept looking at them, as if they expected more.

"We wanted to keep our private lives and our professional ones separate," Kit added.

"The whole thing reminded us of a stunt we pulled when we were first married," Arthur said, smiling fondly at Harriet.

"I was working for Lombardi Foods then," Harriet said, taking up the story. "At a hundred a week, if you can believe it. Anyway, this job opened up, perfect for Arthur. Only they still had nepotism rules.''

"Of course, you couldn't get away with that now,'' Arthur said. "But I needed the job, so I said I was Harriet's husband's second cousin twice removed, or some fool thing like that.''

"Then old man Lombardi caught us kissing in the supply closet.'' Harriet giggled and put her hand up to her cheek.

"Lombardi fired us both on the spot,'' Arthur said. "He told us we were immoral. We never told him we were married to each other.''

Kit smiled at both the Winstons. "Something similar happened to us,'' she said without thinking. "Except...'' She turned to Ryan, met his dark gaze and forgot what she was going to say. He was remembering that moment, too. She could see it in his face. She would have kissed him. She would have initiated the whole thing, if Cynthia hadn't walked in when she had.

"Except we hadn't quite reached the kissing part,'' Ryan said, slipping his arm behind her along the sofa and stroking the back of her neck.

She gazed at him. What was he doing? He'd already short-circuited her brain with a single glance, and now he was assuring her complete mental breakdown by caressing the nape of her neck. It would feel so good simply to close her eyes and enjoy the sensual warmth of his fingers. She jerked her gaze back to the Winstons.

"So,'' she said as brightly as she could muster. So? Why had she said that? She didn't have a thing to say.

A short silence fell over the four of them, then Harriet said, "How did you two meet?''

"How did we meet?'' Kit echoed. Ryan was still deliciously tormenting her with delicate strokes of his fingers. If he could affect her this much by touching her neck in public, what if they were alone and had the freedom to touch wherever they pleased?

"What she really wants to know is how did you fall in love and get married," Arthur said with a wink at his wife.

"Well, you want to know, too," Harriet said to her husband. "Don't deny it."

He didn't deny it, and they both sat there with bright, expectant looks on their very similarly round faces, as if having such personal conversations with people they hardly knew was a very ordinary thing. But Kit knew that getting their contract meant Ryan's keeping his job. So she probably should tell them what they wanted to know. If only she could focus her attention and think of a reasonable answer.

"It was love at first sight," Ryan said. "But we didn't know it until third or maybe fourth sight."

"That's so sweet," Harriet said.

Kit turned and stared at him. It was true, absolutely true. And she hadn't realized it until now. Of course, she'd fallen in love with him the moment she'd seen him. But how could he have known that?

Ryan returned her gaze, a smoky look in his dark eyes. "Your turn," he said.

She forced herself to look at Arthur and Harriet. What should she say? Wait, what was that rule—stick to the truth when telling a lie? "We met at a wedding. Ryan was best man, and I was maid of honor."

"She caught the bouquet," Ryan said. "But she didn't want it, so she gave it to me and told me that we were meant for each other. The next thing I knew, we were a married couple."

"Are you saying *she* proposed to *you?*" Arthur asked with raised eyebrows.

Kit turned to stare at Ryan. He wouldn't tell them she'd proposed, would he?

"It wasn't so much a proposal as an executive order," Ryan said with a grin.

That was all the Winstons needed. They laughed and whooped and chortled, while Kit felt the heat of embarrassment creep up her neck.

Kit paced the length of the bedroom the Winstons had assigned them for their visit. They had only a few minutes' grace before they had to appear downstairs for dinner, and she intended to make it perfectly clear to Ryan that he wasn't to invent any more stories for the Winstons' delectation. So where was he? He and Arthur had gone off to survey the small winery Arthur had built behind the house, while Harriet had shown Kit the many rooms that made up their country house. But he should be back by now.

She couldn't believe he'd said that she'd ordered him to marry her. It was so insulting. Especially after he'd claimed it had been love at first sight for both of them. And all the time he'd been touching her neck and making her feel all warm and melty inside. Tricking her into thinking maybe he cared for her, too.

She stopped in the middle of the room. She should try to calm down. Men tended not to take you seriously if you appeared too emotional, especially when they were in the wrong. She took several deep breaths. That was much better. She was perfectly calm.

The door opened and Ryan stepped into the room. "Hi, honey, I'm back," he said, for whose benefit she couldn't imagine. There were just the two of them in the room.

"Don't you honey me," she snapped.

He looked at her wide-eyed. "What did I do?"

"As if you didn't know."

"Well, I don't know. So if you'd just calm down and tell me in a rational manner, maybe I could do something about it."

She raised her chin. "I am perfectly calm."

"Right. And I'm Uncle Sam."

She pointed her finger at him. "You said that I ordered you to marry me."

"First of all, don't shake your finger at me. My mother always did that, and I hate it. Second of all, I said no more than the truth. You told me we had to pretend we were married, and you gave me no say in the matter. Right?"

"You didn't have to tell them that. You could have made up any story at all."

"They loved it. It's just the kind of thing they like to hear."

"Well, I didn't love it. It made me sound cold and managing."

Ryan's expression softened. "Is that what this is about?"

"Of course, haven't you been listening to me?"

"Is there anything else? Let's get it all out in the open."

She drew herself up. Might as well deal with the situation straight on. "I didn't like the way you were tickling my neck."

"Really? I didn't realize you were ticklish," he said, and passed his hand across his mouth as if he was trying to hide a smile.

"Are you laughing at me?"

He put up his hands like a police suspect. "Not guilty,

I swear.'' He closed the space between them and lowered his hands onto her shoulders. "If I smile, it's only because you're so adorable.''

"Humph,'' she snorted. "What a line.''

"It's not a line. Arthur thought you were delightful. He told me so.''

She wasn't going to give in on this one, even if he was standing so close she had to tip her head back to look at him. And when she did that, all she could think was why didn't he bend down and kiss her? "He told you he thought I was delightful?''

"Yes, he did.'' Ryan slipped one hand up to the back of her neck and massaged it gently. "You charmed them both completely, couldn't you tell?''

Her eyes nearly closed. She couldn't help it. "I was so nervous, I couldn't think.'' Ryan had had something to do with her nonthinking condition, too, just as he was now interfering with rational thought by standing so near and stroking her neck.

He bent closer and closer. He was going to kiss her. She closed her eyes completely and offered her mouth to him.

"You know what?'' he said, so close to her she could feel his breath on her lips.

Why was he talking? "What?'' she whispered.

"I don't think you're ticklish at all.''

She opened her eyes and pushed him away. "Oh, you…you…''

"You, what?'' he said, grinning.

"I can't think of a word for it, but it's something awful.''

"I can think of one for you—liar.''

"I am *not* a liar.''

"I beg to differ. Now as for me, I'm being honest

about my feelings. I love your neck. It's so long and graceful, I couldn't stop myself from tracing the line of it. And you looked like a purring cat when I did. But the next thing I know, you're telling me to stop tickling you.''

"I'm as honest as you are," she protested.

"Prove it."

She stared at him. "What?"

"I said, prove it." He stood at ease with his hands at his sides.

"How?"

"Show me your honest feelings, and I'll show you mine."

"I don't know what you mean."

"Kiss me."

"Kiss you?"

"Please?" He held out his hand.

She looked at his hand, and her hand, acting on its own, reached out to join with his. She lifted her gaze. His eyes had that smoky look in them again, as if banked fires burned within. An answering warmth spread over her.

"If you want to kiss me," she said, a little breathless, "why didn't you just a minute ago?"

"I wanted you to want to, and not just go along because it was my idea. So the question is, do you want to?"

It really wasn't a choice situation. She had only one option. She must kiss him, because every part of her heart and body wanted her to.

She released his hand and slid her arms around his neck. In the next instant she was kissing him with her lips, tongue, hands and every other part of her she could press close to him. He answered her every gesture with one of his own, each one more urgent than the last, until they lost their balance and tumbled onto the bed.

She laughed as they bounced up and down on the springy mattress.

"I love your laugh," Ryan said, and proceeded to kiss the laughter from her lips.

She kissed him back enthusiastically. He loved her neck. He loved her laugh. Could it possibly be that he loved her?

Suddenly he jerked his head up. "Oh, hell, the Winstons." He pushed up on one elbow and looked at his watch. "We were supposed to be downstairs five minutes ago."

He lowered his face to her neck. She could feel his lips through the tangle of her hair, undone from its pins in their tussle on the bed. "I love your hair," he murmured against her neck.

She closed her eyes and smiled. Laugh, neck and now hair—maybe he was going to declare himself to each part individually. Hadn't anyone ever told him that the whole was greater than the sum of its parts? She opened her eyes, pulled a few inches away from Ryan and gazed at his incredibly handsome, sexy face. Should she tell him she loved him? Maybe he was holding back from saying it because he wasn't sure of her.

"What's going on behind those green eyes of yours?" he asked.

"I was wondering how long the Winstons would hold dinner before they came looking for us."

"Good God!" He pushed himself to a sitting position. "I remembered, then I forgot completely. You have the most incredible effect on me. Do you know that?"

She didn't answer. She had a question of her own that

had to do with the two of them and forever, but she'd look for the answer later, after dinner.

Dinner with the Winstons passed in painful slow motion. Ryan found a thousand occasions to check his watch surreptitiously—while cutting his meat, passing the salt or straightening his napkin in his lap—but the hands stubbornly refused to move forward more than a few meager minutes at a time.

He could have gladly wolfed down his food and excused himself from the table like a teenager off on a hot date. But, although the Winstons dined early when they were in the country, they didn't finish early, and course after course was brought in and lingered over.

He complimented Harriet Winston on her chef—twice. He'd forgotten he'd already said something until he'd started praising him the second time. Judging from the quizzical look on Harriet's face, he must have used the same words both times.

Kit gazed at him from the other side of the table and gave a little shake of her head like a warning. But warnings did no good. He was beyond help, because she was a green-eyed, red-haired temptress who had made him forget everything except his desire for her.

As soon as dessert arrived at the table, Arthur finally turned the conversation to the issue of the contract with Calvert. Curious, he asked what it was like for the two of them to work together.

Kit must have guessed by now that Ryan was less than useless when it came to coherent conversation, so she pitched right in with the truth. They'd scrapped like cats and dogs, she told them.

He wouldn't put it that strongly, Ryan protested.

How would he put it, she wanted to know? Of course,

they'd done a lot of their fighting on E-mail, so no one would know that they disagreed on every major aspect. She knew how important the heavier gauge of metal and four-color design were to the kind of container the Winstons wanted for their product. He'd harassed her with budget restraints, tight production schedules and the need to come up with a reasonable bid.

Why had she decided to be truthful in this instance, when the rest of their dealings with the Winstons were strewn with lies? But the Winstons ate it up and came back for more. And the evening came to an end at last with much shaking of hands and sly looks from both Harriet and Arthur as Ryan ushered Kit out of the room.

Ryan had his arm around Kit's waist as they mounted the stairs to their room. He was hurrying, on the verge of running, until Kit said, "Not so fast, please."

He slowed down a fraction. He wouldn't go too fast for her, not up the stairs and not into bed. He had all the time in the world, because this woman was worth the wait.

He had to drop his arm so they could pass one by one through the bedroom door. He made sure the bedroom door was tightly shut and turned to face her. Now, at last, he had her all to himself, and for a whole night. He moved toward her. Their third night together, but their first real night with each other.

"Congratulations," she said, smiling at him. "You did it."

He stopped in his tracks. "What did I do?"

"You got the contract, of course."

"So that's what all that handshaking and backslapping was about just now."

She frowned at him. "Are you all right?"

He felt a smile spread over his whole face. "Never better." He wanted to grab her and kiss her silly, but she looked a little uncertain. He'd better take it slow.

"I thought you'd be happy about it," she said. "It's why we're here. John won't fire you now."

"I am happy about it. But I think we're here for another reason, too." He held out his hand. "A much more important reason."

She gave him a long look that let him read all the desire she felt for him written in her face. In the next instant she was in his arms. The feel of her warm body leaning against his was more inebriating than the rare vintage wines Arthur Winston had poured out for them at dinner. He sought her lips with his. The instant his mouth touched hers, a firestorm broke out between them. He had to touch her all over, caress her, possess her, if only they both weren't wearing so many clothes.

He worked at the buttons on her blouse while never letting his lips leave hers. When the last button slipped free, he broke off their kissing long enough to gaze at her. She was breathing hard through parted lips, looking like a well-kissed woman who wanted nothing more than to be kissed some more. Her unbuttoned blouse revealed creamy white breasts barely covered by a lacy bra.

"You are so beautiful," he breathed. "Did I ever tell you that before?"

She shook her head.

He raised a hand to her breast and traced the border where the lace left off and her skin began. "I'm very remiss. I should have told you a thousand times by now. You are so beautiful."

"Ryan," she whispered, "I..." She broke off and bit her lip.

He smiled at her. She was passionate, but she was shy,

too. "Hush," he said. "It's all right. I know how you feel."

"You do?" she asked, her eyes all bright intensity.

"Yes, I do. It shows quite clearly. And I want you to know that I feel exactly the same way about you."

"Oh, Ryan." She threw herself into his arms and kissed him with more fire than he'd ever experienced. He'd wanted to take it slow with her, but she was making it impossible. He freed one of her arms from around his neck and started to slip her arm out of her sleeve.

"Wait," she said against his mouth.

He pulled back and gazed into her eyes. "Did you say—wait?"

"Just a minute, that's all. I want tonight to be perfect."

"We have the recipe and the ingredients for perfection right here," he said, and tried to pull her arm free of the other sleeve.

"Yes, but I'd like to go in there." She waved in the direction of the bathroom. "It won't take me long."

He released her. "Right. Of course."

She smiled at him and touched his face with her fingers. "I'll be right back."

"I'll be waiting," he said, and watched as she picked up her suitcase and disappeared into the bathroom. He'd be waiting, all right. He'd wait a thousand years, because she was so exquisite and so desirable. Or, at the very least, he'd try to wait for as long as she needed, but even a few minutes felt like torture.

He looked around the room. She wanted perfection. He'd do his best to give it to her. He crossed to the bedside and turned on the lamp and switched off the overhead. What else was there? The bed covers remained to be pulled back, and that took but a second. And, of course, his own clothes still needed to be removed. Coat, tie, shoes and socks flew into the corner of the room. He had just finished unbuttoning his shirt when the bathroom door opened.

She stood framed in the doorway, smiling uncertainly at him. She wore a wisp of a nightgown, a tantalizing drape of green satin that hung on her shoulders by the thinnest straps and ended midthigh. Her hair curled around her head and hung to her shoulders like a cloud of fire.

"Mercy," he croaked.

She smiled wider and crossed to him with a confident sway of her hips. "You like it?" she asked, sliding her hands up his chest.

He put his hands on her waist, but the slick material encouraged him to slide them down her hips. "It's sort of a love-hate thing. I like it, but not on you. Right now I couldn't like anything on you."

"All right." She crossed to the bed and stretched out with her head resting against the headboard. "But you go first."

He tore at his shirt, pulling it from his shoulders, but the sleeves caught on his hands, because he'd forgotten to unbutton the cuffs. He looked down at the inside-out sleeves dangling from his hands and back up at Kit, who watched him with a little smile playing around her mouth.

She sat up and motioned him to the bed. "Here, let me help."

"How embarrassing," he said, sitting down on the edge of the bed. "Not the suave lover at all."

She fixed his shirt and unfastened his cuffs. "I don't want a suave lover. I want you."

He tossed his shirt aside and pulled her across his lap. "You know just the right things to say, don't you," he said.

"I was a little afraid to say what I was feeling before."

"But you can say it now, right? We don't have to be shy around each other."

She smiled with such radiance he had to blink twice. God, but she was beautiful.

"I can say it now. I love you, Ryan."

That wasn't quite what he had expected to hear, but he liked the sound of it, anyway. She loved him. She belonged to him. He liked that feeling a lot. He nibbled on her ear and whispered, "And I adore you."

She held quite still for a few seconds.

"You okay?" he asked, abandoning her ear.

"I was wondering. Have you any thoughts about the future? I mean, our future?"

"Yes," he said. "I have very definite and explicit thoughts about the immediate future." He addressed himself to her neck and shoulders. He'd never seen such fine skin, like silk against his mouth.

"I meant after tonight? Did you have any thoughts about us—together?"

He lifted his head and gazed at her. "Of course I have. You don't think this is just a one-night stand, do you?"

"No, I don't."

He lifted a hand to stroke her cheek. She needed reassurance, and he could give it to her. "I don't want be apart from you, Kit."

She relaxed her body against his and smiled at him. "That's how I feel," she said.

"I've even thought this through. Since everyone already thinks we're married, we might as well let them go on thinking it."

She went rigid in his arms. "We might as well?"

"Sure, we can pick whose apartment works best and

move in together. Or, maybe rent something bigger. Whatever you like.''

She pushed herself out of his arms, slid off his lap and stood up.

''Kit?'' He stood up and reached for her, but she eluded his grasp. Maybe he was going too fast for her, talking about moving in together. ''What's the matter?''

She wrapped her arms around herself. ''I don't want to pretend.''

He rose to his feet. ''You don't want to pretend to be married? That's okay with me. We'll tell everyone we're not married. Only, you'll have to tell Warren and Mary.''

She gazed at him with solemn eyes. ''I didn't mean that. I meant that I want us to be together forever and ever. I want to be married to you.''

''You what?'' He put his hands on his hips. ''Wait a minute. You told me more than once that you were never going to get married.''

She made a small shrugging gesture, and one of the thin straps of her nightgown slipped off her shoulder. He reached for her again, but she pulled back and wouldn't let him touch her.

''Why are you doing this?'' he asked.

''Because I love you.''

''And I'm crazy about you. Isn't that enough?''

''I'm not sure. Would you say it's a full-blown psychosis or just a nagging neurosis?'' She turned on her heel, marched into the bathroom and flipped on the light. Through the open doorway he could see her rummaging in her suitcase.

''What the hell are you doing?''

She pulled on a pair of slacks and tucked her nightgown into the waistline without answering him.

"You're putting on your clothes because I said I was crazy about you, but I don't want to get married?"

She pulled a sweater over her head. "Yes, but I don't expect you to understand." She stuffed her bare feet into her shoes.

"Of course not, because what you're doing is incomprehensible."

"That's what I said. You wouldn't understand."

"You'd better watch out who you go around calling psychotic, you know, because you're the one who's acting crazy."

She fastened her bag and picked it up.

"What are you doing?"

"Leaving."

"In the middle of the night? How are you going to get back to San Francisco—walk?"

"If I have to."

He dug his keys out of his pocket and separated the car keys from the ring. "Take my car."

She looked at the keys and didn't move. "But how will you get back?"

"What do you care?" He held out the keys. "Do me a favor. Take them and get out of here. Park it near your apartment. I have another set of keys. We won't even have to see each other."

He turned away from her and waited until he heard the click of the door closing behind her. Damn. What was wrong with her? Whatever it was, he was well out of it now, because she could only make his life a living hell if he let her keep playing these games with him. He slumped down on the bed. Good thing he'd found out in time. A very good thing. If he kept saying it over and over, he might convince himself by morning.

Chapter Ten

Kit tried to catch the heavy front door of her apartment building before it crashed shut, but her timing was off, and it slammed with a thunk. Predictably, within seconds, Mrs. Grady, the building manager, opened her door and peeked out. Kit hefted her overnight bag, ducked her head and started toward her own apartment. She just couldn't face anyone right now, not even dear, old, lonely Mrs. Grady.

"Kit, is that you?"

Kit halted and slowly swung around. "You're up pretty late, Mrs. Grady. It's after three in the morning."

"It's not late for me," she said, pulling her bathrobe more tightly around her. "You know I haven't slept a wink since my Joe died."

Kit knew for a fact that Mrs. Grady had been a widow for more than twenty years. It seemed a pretty long time for grief-inspired insomnia to last. She intended to get over Ryan more quickly than that. The next twenty minutes would do very nicely.

Mrs. Grady eyed Kit's suitcase. "You're back from your weekend early, aren't you?"

Kit didn't answer, but Mrs. Grady must have noticed something of what Kit was feeling, because she didn't pursue her question. "Some packages came for you," she said. "They have your apartment number on them, all right, but they're addressed to someone else." She bustled back into her apartment, leaving the door open.

"I'll deal with it tomorrow, Mrs. Grady," Kit called after her, but Mrs. Grady didn't hear.

She reappeared in the doorway carrying three fair-sized packages. "They're addressed to Mr. and Mrs. Ryan Holt. Are they staying with you?"

Kit took the packages without answering the question and all the other questions that lurked in Mrs. Grady's bright eyes. "Thanks, Mrs. Grady. Hope you get some sleep."

"You know what they say about men, don't you? Can't live with them and can't live without them."

"You know what else they say? If we can put one man on the moon, why not put all of them there?"

Mrs. Grady patted Kit's arm. "Like that, is it, dear?"

"In spades. Good night. Thanks for taking delivery on the packages for me." Kit walked down the hall. When she reached her own apartment, she balanced packages, suitcase and purse in order to get the keys in the lock and the door opened. Once she'd turned on the light, she waved to Mrs. Grady, who always watched until she was safely inside her apartment. Kit had never managed to bring herself to ask directly how a seventy-year-old who was on the small side intended to protect Kit if someone had attacked her.

She dumped her suitcase on the floor and the packages on the sofa. The tape on one of them had come loose. It would take the merest tug to pull it completely off, not that she wanted to open it. She wasn't Mrs. Ryan Holt and never would be. But somehow her hand took hold of the tape and pulled it free. Then there was nothing for it but to open the flaps of the carton. Inside, nestled in a bed of foam peanuts, lay a box wrapped in silver paper decorated with white wedding bells.

She turned away and stared blankly at the wall. Of all the things she couldn't face right now, wedding presents came near the top of the list, right after Ryan Holt.

''I never want to see him again,'' she said aloud. If she said it over and over again, she might even begin to believe it.

Ryan pulled his chair closer to his desk and scanned the production figures on his computer screen. He'd come in to work early today so he could get this report out first thing, but so far he hadn't accomplished much. He rubbed his hands over his face. He could use a cup of coffee, but the coffee was on Kit's side of the building, and he wasn't sure he was ready to see her, not after this weekend.

How had everything gone so wrong? One minute she was in his arms all soft and sultry, and the next she was walking out the door. He massaged his temples. He hadn't had much sleep that night. Or the next one, either. He'd been angry at her, but couldn't seem to stay mad. Images of her kept creeping into his brain. No woman had ever obsessed him the way she did. When awake, he thought about her even when he didn't want to, and when asleep, well, the sooner those erotic dreams were drowned in a cold shower, the better.

He pushed away from his desk and stood up. If only she hadn't pulled that marriage thing on him. What had prompted that, anyway? She'd been so adamant on the marriage issue before that she hadn't even wanted to pretend to be married for the Winstons. And she knew how he felt about it. Marriage simply wasn't for him. At least, not now.

He crossed to the window and peered out at the fog wisping across the parking lot. If they were married, they'd be tied, chained, bound to each other. If he got another job offer, she'd have to agree to the move, or they couldn't go. And what about when he wanted to start his own business, what then? She wouldn't want to take the risk. It would tie up all their capital, including the down payment on the house she'd be sure to want.

He'd been over this ground before—repeatedly, in fact, since their blowup Saturday night. But it seemed harder to hang on to his rational conviction when he kept getting sidetracked by thoughts of Kit. Maybe wanting to get married was just a temporary thing with her. She'd said she loved him. Maybe they could still work things out.

At the knock on his door, he turned around. Kit walked in before he could invite her to and closed the door behind her. She looked pale and a little haggard, like someone who hadn't slept well, but no less desirable than she'd been in his imaginings for the past two days.

He'd deliberately avoided running into her this morning, but now he couldn't quite remember why. "Hello, Kit."

"I'm sorry to interrupt you, but I need to talk to you about something." Her gaze drifted away from him, and she twisted her fingers together, the third finger on her left hand now noticeably bare.

"I see you've taken off your wedding ring," he said.

She winced as if in pain, and he quickly looked away.

God knew he didn't want to hurt her. He just wanted…
her.

"It isn't mine. It belongs to Lindsay, remember?" she
said, giving each word a tart emphasis and tilting her chin
to that familiar, belligerent angle.

He smiled. He couldn't help himself. She drew it out
of him just by standing there and making waspish com-
ments. Just by sticking out her chin and looking so beautiful. Just by being Kit. "Yes, how could I forget?" he
said, and smiled some more.

He moved toward her. He didn't want to, but he didn't
know how not to. What was it about her that held him
so? Involuntarily, his hand reached out toward her.

She gave him such a look then, with hurt and scorn
mixed in equal measures, that he jerked his hand back to
his side as quickly as if he'd scorched it.

"I want a divorce," she said.

Divorce—the word came at him like a blow to the solar
plexus. "What?"

"You can skip the irony. You needn't remind me
we're not really married."

"No, I'm sure I don't," he murmured. No need to
remind her, but what about him? He turned and moved
back behind his desk. Why was he so shocked? He didn't
want to be married. Nothing could be more certain. But
hell, he didn't want to lose her, either.

"The problem is that I've received wedding presents,"
she said.

"I see," he said, not actually seeing anything at all
except that she wanted to make a complete break with
him. That might be for the best, but how could he stand
it?

"I think we should make some kind of public statement."

He rubbed the back of his neck. "Wouldn't it be simpler to send the presents back?"

"Of course I'll send them back. But don't you see? It's just the beginning. We'll get more and more presents. You don't know how many friends Mary and Warren have."

"Well, you're welcome to use my phone if you want to put out a company-wide message. How should we word it? Kit and Ryan are not now, nor have they ever been, married?"

It was a weak attempt at humor, and it only served to bring color to her cheeks and increase the tilt of her chin. "I think we need to reach a wider audience than the employees here at Calvert."

"Why do I have the feeling that you already have a plan? Just tell me what it is."

"Deborah Waterston invited us to a big bash. I knew her from school, and I've stayed friendly because Deborah has a hefty trust fund and makes large contributions to Mary's charities."

"Let me see if I can interpret that. This Deborah isn't a particular friend, but you stay on her good side for Mary's sake."

"That's about it."

"Then why would we want to go to her party?"

"Because it will be written up in the social news."

"I see. And what do we do? Ask everyone to be quiet while we make our announcement?"

"We wouldn't have to do that. I could call and explain that we'd both like to come to the party, but not with each other, because we're getting a divorce."

"What do you mean 'not with each other'?"

"I thought we should each show up with dates, but

still be friendly to each other. Then Mary and Warren would hear about it and know we're both okay.''

He stared at her. How could he possibly be okay if she was going out with another man? ''I don't think that's such a good idea.''

''Do you have a better one?''

He tugged at the collar of his shirt. ''What if we gave this thing another try?''

''What 'thing' is that?''

''You know, you and me.'' He moved from behind his desk and crossed to her. ''You know I really do…care about you. A lot. And I know you care about me. Why don't we try to work out a compromise or something?''

Her face softened for the first time since she'd come into his office, and she looked sad enough to cry. ''Because you're asking me to make a choice between being hurt now or destroyed later.'' She moved toward the door. ''The party's Friday night at eight. I'll send you directions.''

''Wait.'' He loosened his tie. It was so hot in his office, he was sweating. ''Look, you want to get married. Okay, let's get married.'' There, he'd said it. Let her have it her way. At least she wouldn't be leaving him, going out with someone else. The bottom line was, he couldn't bear to lose her. That was all that mattered right now.

She put her fists on her hips. ''You are the most arrogant, conceited, unfeeling person I have ever met. How I ever could have thought I was in love with you is beyond me.''

''What are you talking about? I thought you wanted to get married.''

''There's no point in explaining. You wouldn't understand. See you Friday night. Bring a date.'' She pulled the door open and marched out with a toss of her flame red hair.

He stared at the empty doorway. That was absolutely it. He wasn't going to have anything more to do with Kit, no matter what. The woman was completely nuts. So he'd been attracted to her. Okay, more than attracted. She mattered to him, but that was over now. He would put it behind him. There were other women as attractive, as dynamic, as adorable—he just hadn't met any of them yet.

Kit let the maid take her coat and turned to Jeremy. "Thanks so much for bringing me tonight. I know you must have had other plans but were too nice to tell me."

"I'm glad you asked me," Jeremy said, his smile a dazzling flash in his handsome face. "What are old former fiancés good for, anyway, if not to show up new former fiancés? Especially jerks like this Ryan Holt."

"He's really not a jerk, and we weren't ever actually engaged," Kit said. It had been a relief to confide in Jeremy. Dear old Jeremy, who'd stayed a close friend even after he'd accepted that she'd never marry him. He'd taken her side with a vehemence that at first pleased her, but now made her uneasy. "You won't try to confront him or anything, will you?"

"I consider it my sworn duty to knock the block off any man who makes you unhappy, Kit. You know that."

"That's very sweet of you. But Ryan and I are trying to show everyone that we're friends. It's important for Mary and Warren's sake."

"All right, I'll be good. But, tell me, how am I supposed to act around you? Am I merely your escort for the night, or do I imply something more by my attentions to you?"

"Just act the way you always do," she said hastily. Maybe asking Jeremy along hadn't been such a good idea. What if he got the idea that just because she'd wanted to marry Ryan, now she'd consider marrying him? "I suppose we'd better stop hiding out here in the hallway and face the crowd."

Jeremy grinned at her. "If I didn't know you better, I'd say you were nervous."

Kit took Jeremy's arm and lifted her chin. "Me, nervous? Don't be sil—" She broke off.

"What's the matter?"

"Nothing, nothing at all." She forced a smile. No point in explaining that Ryan always stopped her when she told him not to be silly. She didn't want to remember those moments. "Let's go."

She clutched Jeremy's arm and kept her head high as they entered Deborah Waterston's elegant Victorian living room, crowded now with wall-to-wall partygoers.

Deborah herself swept up to them. "Kit and Jeremy. Look at you. Just like old times. So glad you could make it. Your very charming ex is already here, Kit. So mature of you to insist on having him invited to the same party. I don't know if I could have done it."

Kit forced herself not to scan the room immediately for a glimpse of Ryan. She smiled back at Deborah. With any luck at all her smile wouldn't look too insincere. Deborah had been one of the girls who used to snub her at school—until Mary and Warren took her in.

"Hello, Deborah," Jeremy said. "Nice party."

"Good to see you, Jeremy. Am I to assume that you and Kit are an item again?"

"You may assume that Jeremy and I are, and will always be, best of friends," Kit said.

"That's nice," Deborah said in that way she had of

making it sound like she meant the complete opposite. "Ryan came with a 'friend' as well, a very friendly friend, if you know what I mean. I believe her name is Cynthia." Deborah let the name hang in the air and peered into Kit's face.

Kit stared back at Deborah unblinking. She'd be darned if she'd let any reaction show. "Yes, I know," she lied with a smile, and took Jeremy's arm. "Don't let us keep you from your other guests. Jeremy and I can mingle on our own." She held her smile in place and jerked Jeremy into action next to her.

"Careful with the arm," Jeremy said as they swung away from Deborah. "I steer better by voice command."

Kit ignored him and let her gaze roam over the crowd. "I can't believe he brought her."

"You mean Cynthia? Who is she?"

"My assistant, the little traitor," she said between gritted teeth. "Hi, there," she said to someone whose name escaped her, and kept moving, dragging Jeremy along with her.

"I thought the idea was that you'd both come with dates and show everyone how amicably you've parted."

"Zip it, Jeremy. You know I hate it when you get that reasonable tone."

"Sorry. Give me a moment, and I'll work up something completely irrational."

They wove their way around the chatting guests, Kit smiling, but not stopping to chat with anyone who tried to get her attention. Where was Ryan, anyway?

"I have it," Jeremy said. "She's really unattractive and that will reflect badly on you."

"She's very young," Kit said. "And she's disgustingly enthusiastic about everything. She has this curly brown hair that bounces around all the time because she's bubbling about something or other.''

"Just what I thought—a veritable hag with no discernible personality. You will introduce me, though, won't you?''

"You want to meet her? Why?''

"I can't imagine,'' he said. "Put it down to sheer perversity.''

She spotted Ryan at just that moment. Or maybe he'd seen her first and drew her attention by the power of his gaze. She stared at him, frozen where she stood. Would every time she saw him be like this? Or would she get used to the overpowering yearning to run right into his arms and beg him to let her stay for as long as he'd have her?

"So that's Ryan, hmm?'' Jeremy said softly in her ear.

Kit forced herself to look away. "Yes. How did you guess?''

Jeremy gave her a pitying look. "Face it, Kit. You love him. You know it, and now so does anyone in the room who's been watching you two.''

"You're wrong. I hate him.''

Jeremy slipped his arm around her waist and leaned toward her. "Hang on to that thought, because here they come.''

She hadn't a second to organize her thoughts, because Ryan was standing right in front of her, with Cynthia hanging on to his arm as if she owned it.

"Hello, Kit,'' Ryan said.

Just the sight of him made her mouth dry up and her heart crash around in her chest. And she couldn't even look at Cynthia. How was she going to pull off ordinary conversation?

Jeremy leapt into the breach by holding out his hand and saying, "You must be Ryan. I'm Jeremy."

Ryan stared hard at Jeremy's face, then down at his hand before he shook it. "Jeremy. Let me see. Where have I heard that name before? I think I was given the use of a pair of your sweatpants when we stayed at the Franklins' Tahoe house."

"Really? I must confess I've never missed them, but I'm happy if you got some use out of them."

Ryan gave him a wry smile. "They weren't what I expected to be wearing on my wedding night, but then, nothing about my marriage to Kit has been particularly normal." His gaze met Kit's, and the words of the crushing riposte she'd assembled in her brain mixed themselves into a hopeless scramble.

A heavy silence followed. Jeremy turned to Cynthia. "I'm Jeremy, and you, I've been told, are Cynthia. Are you enjoying the party?"

How like Jeremy to try to smooth things over. He really was a nice person. Too nice, in fact. Why couldn't he be a little less pleasant? Especially to Cynthia, who'd probably had her eye on Ryan from the first.

"Yes, it's a way cool party," Cynthia said, her hair doing its bouncing thing with nearly every word. "And this house is as big as a mansion. Have you ever seen anything so huge?" Her eyes were wide in wonder.

Jeremy and Ryan both smiled at Cynthia indulgently.

Kit pressed her lips together. "In fact, he's seen many houses this size and larger," she said in her most snubbing manner. "His own house, for one."

Cynthia's mouth formed a little O, but no sound came out.

Jeremy still had his arm around her waist, and he gave her a poke in the ribs. She didn't look at him. So she wasn't acting the role of former spouse who's on friendly terms with her ex. So what? She didn't feel like being friendly. She felt like tugging on one of Cynthia's bouncing brown curls until she howled in pain, which was nothing compared to what she felt like doing to Ryan.

Jeremy dropped his arm from her waist and spoke to Cynthia. "You know what? These two have a few things to discuss, so why don't you and I go and explore the buffet?"

"Jeremy, what are you doing?" Kit protested.

"I'm helping you show the world that you two are parting on amicable terms. Cynthia and I will be back shortly."

She watched Jeremy and Cynthia disappear into the crowd. A number of people turned to cast inquisitive looks in her direction, some more discreetly than others, but all clearly curious. Jeremy was right. She had to give at least the appearance of being on friendly terms with Ryan. She turned to face him again.

"Maybe Jeremy isn't such a sure bet for your future matrimonial plans," Ryan said before she could could get a word out. "He couldn't keep his eyes off Cynthia."

Kit gritted her teeth. And she'd been worried about letting her feelings show. When he talked like that, she almost forgot how much she loved him. "You can keep your sarcasm to yourself. Jeremy is my very dear friend."

"Is he? Well, he's a braver man than I am."

"Yes, he has many positive qualities that you lack."

"Now, what could those be?" He drew his brows together and put his index finger on his chin in an absurd charade of someone puzzling out a problem. "The mansion, for one, I'd guess, and of course, the bank account to go along with it. Once you're married, you can throw your own elaborate parties," he said, gesturing to the spacious room filled with noisy partygoers. "And get written up in the social news."

"If you think I care about any of those things, then you don't know me at all."

"I know all I need to know about you. You're a walking contradiction and nothing but trouble for any man."

Over Ryan's shoulder she saw two people turn around and stare, openly eavesdropping. She smiled at them and waved a greeting. They quickly averted their eyes. She kept the smile on her face and returned her gaze to Ryan. "Do me a favor and stifle your antagonism for a few minutes," she said quietly, "so we can act as if we're friends. That's the whole point of this exercise, you may remember."

He leaned toward her and said softly, "Let's get this straight, Kit. I'm not the only one who's antagonistic here. It's one thing to launch into me, but you were pretty rude to Cynthia. She came with me tonight only as a favor to you."

"A favor to me? How gullible do you think I am? I suppose you also have some swampland you'd like me to invest in."

He straightened and stared at her. "You're jealous."

"Now you're being ridiculous."

"I don't think so." He moved closer to her until she had to tip her head back to look at him.

It was dangerous for her to be this close to him. He'd already passed that critical distance at which she couldn't resist the force of attraction and would surely fly into his arms, like iron to a magnet.

"God, Kit," he said, his voice husky, "when you look at me like that it just about sends me over the edge."

Why, oh why, did she have to love him so? Her life had been simpler before he'd walked into it. Simple and bare, like a tree in winter. She needed to get away from him, before she forgot that he didn't love her, didn't want her forever and ever. Or, she'd just end up plunged back into winter. "I don't think you're in any real danger," she said, and took a step back only to bump into someone behind her.

She mumbled, "I'm sorry," and turned to the person she'd stepped on. Darn...Deborah.

Deborah smiled and raised her eyebrows. "My fault. I should have warned you I was approaching, though I'm not sure you would have heard me."

Kit got her social smile back on her face. Thank goodness for a rescuer. Maybe she could fob Ryan off on Deborah and make a break for home. "Yes, it's a little noisy in here. Ryan, you met Deborah when you arrived, didn't you?"

Ryan smiled perfunctorily at Deborah and nodded.

"Yes, we've met," Deborah said. "And I have to say I was very sorry to hear that you two are divorcing. I know you'll tell me that it's none of my business, but is there any chance of a reconciliation?"

Kit opened her mouth to say absolutely not, but Ryan got in first. "Yes, there's a distinct possibility," he said.

Kit stared at him. Why had he said that? He was going to ruin the whole thing.

"I'm so glad," Deborah said, grasping each of them by the hand. "You know, I'm not the only one who's noticed that there's still quite a bit of chemistry between the two of you, if you know what I mean."

Kit winced. Any minute now, Deborah would be going wink-wink, nudge-nudge. "We're still friends, Deborah, but that's all."

"That's a very good place to start," Deborah replied. "Have you considered seeing a marriage counselor?"

"We haven't," Ryan said. "But maybe we should."

"I don't think it would make any difference," Kit added quickly.

"You don't know until you try," Deborah said, and joined Kit's hand to Ryan's.

His hand enfolded hers, the warmth of his touch streaking up her arm like electricity. He smiled into her eyes. "I think Deborah's right, Kit. Let's get away from this crowd and talk it over." He turned to Deborah. "You'll excuse us, won't you?"

Deborah gave a little trill of laughter. "Of course. Don't mind me."

Ryan pulled her along behind him through the crowd. She tried to tug her hand free from his grip, but he held on and kept moving forward out the door to the wide, wood-paneled hall. She didn't want to go with him, really she didn't. They were supposed to be divorcing, not reconciling.

Ryan kept going till he found a nook between the front hall and the kitchen. It wasn't exactly private, but it was a heck of a lot better than that room with about a hundred of Kit's socialite friends watching them. He stopped and turned to face her, but kept her hand clasped in his. He wasn't going to let her get away. Not this time.

Kit looked up at him with an accusing gaze. "What do you think you're doing?" she demanded.

"Trying to salvage my sanity."

"Well, you're not doing a very good job of it. You're acting quite crazy, you know." She tried to pry his fingers loose with her free hand.

He captured that hand, too, with his other hand and imprisoned both of hers against his chest. Maybe feeling the pounding of his heart quieted her, because at last she held still.

"You make me crazy, Kit. Just the sight of you dazzles me, and I don't know where I am or what I'm doing, except that I want you."

She shook her head as if to deny what he said. "We should go back to the party."

"No. We need to settle this. I don't want you to run away from me. Tell me what it will take to make you stay."

"Oh, Ryan," she said, and her eyes welled up with tears. "Don't, please don't."

"Don't what? Desire you so much I think I'm going to burn up?"

"It's just desire. It will pass."

He pulled her closer. "Will it? Has it for you? Because I know you want me as much as I want you. If I kissed you now, would you feel nothing?"

Her eyes softened, the way they did when she wanted to be kissed. She did want him. He bent his head toward her. She didn't move or try to struggle. Why would she, anyway? She'd told him before that she loved him. That meant he had a claim on her.

Voices in the hallway, then just one voice. "Kit?"

"Jeremy," Kit breathed, and wrenched herself free.

Jeremy stepped into the nook. His eyes flashed from Kit to Ryan and back to Kit. "You okay?" he asked, holding out a hand to her as if he had the right, damn him.

"She's fine," Ryan growled, taking a step toward the other man.

But Kit turned away. "Take me home. I want to go home."

"Sure, Kit," Jeremy said, wrapping an arm around her shoulders.

"I'll take you home," Ryan said. "Let me take you." He would, too, right after he ripped that guy's face off.

Kit held up her hand. "No," she said. "I want Jeremy."

Ryan stopped in his tracks. It felt as if someone had just punched him in the chest. What else could cause such a pain in his heart?

"Kit, wait," he said, and followed her into the hall.

She had to have heard him, but she didn't pause.

"Don't go," he said to the empty doorway. "I love you."

Chapter Eleven

Ryan chewed the last bite of his fourth glazed doughnut and took another sip of coffee. "You know," he said to the skinny blond kid behind the counter, "this is the only all-night doughnut shop I found in the city."

The blond kid looked up from the book he was reading and nodded as if he already knew this. "It's the location—right down the hill from the medical center and next to the streetcar and bus stops. We get a lot of business when the shifts change." He went back to his book.

Ryan swiveled his counter seat and surveyed the room. The light from the overhead fluorescent fixtures ricocheted off the Formica counter and chrome deep fryer. When he'd come in, after driving around in the dark for who knows how long, the glare had been enough to make him wish he'd brought his sunglasses. Maybe this was what people meant when they talked about the harsh light of reality.

The darkened plate-glass window reflected a grayish image of the nearly uninhabited shop. He was the lone customer, with emphasis on *lone*. That was real enough for him.

He turned back to the kid behind the counter. "Give me a couple more of the glazed and a refill on the coffee, would you?"

The kid put his book aside and approached Ryan. "Don't you think you've had enough?"

"Pardon?" Had the kid just said what he thought he'd said?

"Do you know what percentage of the total calories of each doughnut comes from fat?"

"What are you, an undercover agent for Richard Simmons?"

The kid shrugged slightly. "Not everyone knows how bad doughnuts are for you." He couldn't be more than seventeen or eighteen, and skinny, too. He looked like he didn't eat much of what he served his customers.

Ryan leaned forward. "Look, I'm ordering from the *à la carte* menu. I want the doughnuts without the lecture."

The kid refilled his coffee cup and got him his doughnuts without further comment. As soon as the plate hit the counter, Ryan picked up one of the doughnuts and took a big bite. It didn't taste quite as good as the first one had. Or the second, third or fourth. He wiped his fingers on a paper napkin. "You try to talk all of your customers out of buying, or just me?"

The kid rested the palms of his hands on the counter. "I hear the nurses and med students who come in here talking about guys with heart attacks or bypasses. It seems to me that the consumer should be informed, especially older guys."

Where did this kid get off calling him an older guy? "I'm thirty-two," Ryan said with emphasis.

The kid nodded as if Ryan had simply confirmed his worst suspicions.

"I don't usually eat like this," Ryan admitted. "It's just that the woman I love walked out on me tonight. With another guy." Why was he defending himself? The words simply came out of him, as if he had to tell someone, anyone, or burst. "He's rich and good-looking—the other guy—and she used to be engaged to him. But she wanted to marry me. She told me so. And I sort of blew it. Okay, not sort of, I completely blew it. Only I didn't know. I didn't realize how much I loved her."

He had to stop, had to stem the flow of words, or he'd be blubbering any minute. He gulped his coffee. It was too hot for anything more than sipping, and he nearly choked on it.

"I'm sorry about your girlfriend," the kid said. "I just don't think you should take it out on your body. But I'm no expert about relationships."

Ryan eyed him over the rim of his cup. Here was his chance to change the conversation and stop his own foolish flow of confidences. "How can that be? A good-looking guy like you?"

"I don't have time. Not for anything serious, anyway. I'm going to college in the fall. I'll be premed, which is tough. Then I have three years of med school after that, plus one to two years of specialization. I'm looking at eight years minimum before I'll be secure enough and have the time for anything long-term."

Ryan stared at the kid. Talk about time warp. He'd talked exactly like that fourteen years ago. He hadn't had time for a serious relationship, because he had to finish college, then secure his first job, and complete his MBA in his spare time. After that, he'd had to move from city to city to get ahead. Getting ahead, that was all that was

important to him. Until now. Until Kit. And now time
had run out.

"Listen to me," Ryan said, leaning forward. "I used
to think like you. Don't fool yourself. You think you're
getting ahead, but you might just be running in place."

The kid took a step back. "Sure, sure, whatever you
say. But why are you telling me? Why don't you tell
your girlfriend? Maybe she'd change her mind about the
other guy."

"You think I haven't tried? I've been by her apartment
three times tonight and called her twice. She won't answer. Or else she spent the night with…" His throat
closed up. For the life of him he couldn't get the name
out. "You know," he mumbled, "the other guy."

"Bummer," the kid said, wincing in a mime of com-
passion. "So what're you going to do? Give up?"

Ryan stared down at the half-eaten doughnut on his
plate. The kid was right. He'd been acting like someone
who'd given up, but he hadn't, and he wouldn't. Not until
he'd found a way to tell Kit exactly how he felt, not until
he'd convinced her to marry him. He lifted his gaze to
the kid on the other side of the counter. "I'm not giving
up. I'm going to get help."

Ryan shifted in the roomy armchair and gazed at Mary
and Warren Franklin's shocked faces. He'd already surprised them plenty by showing up on their doorstep in
the wee hours of the morning. But telling them the whole
story about his and Kit's "marriage" had stunned them
both to complete silence.

"You mean to say that you'd never even met Kit before Lindsay's wedding?" Mary finally asked.

"That's right," he said.

Mary straightened the collar of her bathrobe and gave

Warren a significant look. Significant of what, it was hard to tell, but Warren seemed to understand her meaning, because he nodded twice.

Ryan shifted in his chair again. Of course, they were stunned at his news, and being awakened at such an hour probably made it harder to take it all in. But couldn't they give him some response? He needed their help, and he needed it now.

"I know it's a shock, and you're upset about Lindsay, but…"

"I'm not the least upset about Lindsay," Mary interrupted.

He stared at her. "You're not?"

"Lindsay has always been headstrong and impulsive," Mary said with a dismissive wave of her hand. "I'd always expected that Lindsay would be the one to elope. That's why I was so surprised when you two showed up and said you were married. Kit just isn't like that, except…" she paused and sent Warren another significant look.

Ryan gripped the arms of the chair. Except what? Except with mansion-owning, glamour boys like Jeremy? He gave his head a shake. Kit hadn't married Jeremy before, and she wouldn't now, not if he had anything to say about it.

"Yes?" he prompted.

"Except with you, of course," Mary said. "Are you all right, Ryan? You look a little tense."

"I'm fine," he said automatically, then followed the direction of her gaze to his hands clutching the armrests of the chair. He quickly lifted his hands and rested them in his lap. "I'm not fine, in fact. I need your help."

Warren leaned forward in his seat. "That's what you

said when you came to the door. What kind of help do you need?''

"I want to marry Kit."

Warren relaxed into his chair and smiled. "Glad to hear it. Saves me a trip upstairs to get the twelve gauge."

Ryan swallowed hard. "No need for it, sir, I can assure you."

Mary gave Warren's hand a playful slap. "Don't tease the boy, Warren. You can see how much he loves her." She turned to Ryan. "How soon do you plan on getting married? I hope you're not going to elope this time."

"From the look of him," Warren said with a grin, "I'd guess he wants to get married right away."

"Well, I need an absolute minimum of two weeks," Mary said. "I couldn't do it in anything less. Can you wait two weeks?"

Ryan looked from one to the other. They were wonderful people. He couldn't have invented better in-laws-to-be. So why, when he needed them most, did they have to be so completely exasperating? "You don't understand," Ryan said. "What I've been trying to explain to you is that I want to get married, but I can't get Kit to talk to me."

"But you told us that she said she wanted to marry you," Warren said.

"Yes, but at that moment I wasn't ready. I mean, I just didn't realize how much I loved her, and I said I didn't want to." He rubbed his forehead. Could anything be harder than trying to defend inexcusable actions to Kit's parents?

"And now?" Mary said softly.

"Now I know I can't live without her. I never want to be apart from her—never."

"Well, then," Warren said. He sent a significant look to Mary, and Mary returned it.

That did it. The wall of restraint he'd held against his anxiety and fear of losing Kit crumbled. "'Well, then' what?" he nearly shouted. "Tell me straight out what you think my chances are. You keep exchanging looks. And you know what you mean, but I don't. I was a jerk, and I know it. I hurt her. You should have seen her face. I'll do anything to make it up to her. Just tell me you'll help me."

"My dear," Mary said with her gentle smile. "Of course we'll help. We think you're wonderful. We thought so right from the start. Didn't we, Warren?"

Warren nodded. "True, but what we think is irrelevant."

"Yes, it is," Mary agreed. "It's what Kit thinks that matters. And we know that she loves you. That's why we keep looking at each other. We've wanted this for her for so long."

Ryan gazed at Mary. She was one person he'd swear was incapable of any deception. If she said Kit loved him, then it had to be true. He had to squeeze his eyes shut for a second because of a sudden burning sensation behind his eyelids. He blinked, and the feeling passed.

"I have a plan," he said.

Kit rolled over in bed. Someone was knocking at her front door. It had to be Mrs. Grady—she didn't know anyone else in the building who'd knock on her door this early on a Saturday morning. Maybe if she didn't answer, Mrs. Grady would go away. She closed her eyes.

The knocking persisted. She opened her eyes and sat up. What difference did it make? Sleep was as far away as it had been when she got into bed hours ago. Maybe

Mrs. Grady would be a good distraction. She stumbled out of bed, hauled on her bathrobe and headed for the living room.

"Who is it?" she called through the door.

"It's me," Mrs. Grady called back. "You have a package."

Just what she didn't need—another wedding present. She unlocked the door and opened it. Ryan, his chin in need of a shave and his suit in need of pressing, stood in the hall next to Mrs. Grady. Kit's heart did the bungee cord bounce it always did whenever she saw him.

"Go away," she said, but didn't move to close the door.

"Just give me a minute, Kit," Ryan said.

Kit looked at Mrs. Grady. "You shouldn't have let him in."

Mrs. Grady took the accusation lightly and simply shrugged and smiled.

"We have to decide what to do about this wedding present," Ryan said, holding out a gift-wrapped package. She backed away from it, and the next thing she knew, he'd moved past her into her apartment.

Mrs. Grady winked and said, "I'll be down the hall if you need me."

Kit closed the door and leaned her back against it.

"That's some bodyguard you have there," he said with that disarming smile he used to get his way. He'd probably used it on Mrs. Grady. Well, he wasn't going to get his way with her. She hadn't spent a sleepless night planning how she'd handle being around him at work just to have her resolutions fly out the window the second he showed up in her apartment.

"You don't look too good," she said, giving his wrinkled suit a deliberate once-over.

"You look good enough to kiss," he said, looking her over in turn and scorching her skin wherever his gaze passed.

This wouldn't do. It wouldn't do at all. She stiffened her back and held out her hand. "I'll return the present. Who's it from?"

"That's just the problem," Ryan said, moving toward the sofa. "There wasn't any card, no return address. Nothing." He sat down on the sofa and put the present on the coffee table. "I thought we should open it together and decide what to do about it."

Kit crossed to a chair opposite Ryan. Nothing would persuade her to sit next to him on the sofa, even though he moved to make room for her. Especially because he moved to make room. She'd been over and over this situation in her mind. The very best thing for her was to keep her distance. She'd get over him—eventually. If she put her mind to it. It was just hard to put her mind to it when he was in the same room, leveling that dark gaze at her.

"All right," she said. "Open it. Let's see what it is. Maybe there's a card inside."

He shrugged. "Okay." He made short work of the ribbon and paper, and, in a few seconds, a boxed game of Scrabble sat on the coffee table. It didn't look new, either.

Kit pulled the box toward her and lifted the lid. A notebook labeled Babble lay on top. She looked up at Ryan. "This must have come from Mary and Warren. It's our family game." She gently picked up the notebook and leafed through the first few pages.

"So that's the famous dictionary, huh?" Ryan said.

"What a sweet idea to give this to us," Kit said, still holding the notebook.

"Yeah," he agreed. "The problem is, what do we do with it?"

"What do you mean? We have to return it."

Ryan raised his eyebrows. "They don't want it back. They didn't even send a card with it. I think we have to treat it as community property."

"We don't *have* community property."

"We do now," he said softly.

She narrowed her eyes at him. What was he up to? "I don't want to get into an argument with you, Ryan."

"Okay, tell you what. I'll take it." He reached for the box.

She swiftly pulled the box out of his reach. "You will not. It's my family's game. I'll keep it."

"I don't think that's very fair. I happen to like this game a lot. You already know all the words. I need the book if I'm going to learn them."

"Make up your own darn words. I'm keeping it." She fit the notebook inside the box and replaced the lid.

"I think you're being pretty unreasonable, but tell you what. Let's play for it. Winner gets to keep the game."

"You're kidding," she said with a laugh.

He gave her a grim look. "Believe me, the one thing I'm not doing is kidding."

She blinked. "But you don't have a chance. I'll destroy you. When we played before, I had over twice as many points as you without even trying."

He broke into a sudden grin that shattered the air of seriousness he'd been carrying with him. "Yes, but I'd planned from the start to let you win."

"You're just saying that," she said with a toss of her head.

"If that's what you think, then you shouldn't have any

problem winning again, right?'' He held out his hand. ''Come on, Kit. Let's play. I'll set it up.''

She placed the box between them on the coffee table, leaned back in her chair and folded her arms. This was crazy, but she had to have that game. It was unthinkable to let Ryan take it away from her.

Ryan carefully opened the board and set it on the coffee table. ''Since you're such a proficient player, you won't mind if I go first, will you? It will give me only a slight advantage.'' He picked up the bag that held the letters.

''There's a bigger advantage in going second,'' she said.

''I think, in this case, you're wrong.''

''Ryan, listen to me. I'm going to win by a huge margin. At least give yourself a fighting chance and let me go first.''

She held out her hand for the bag, but he went ahead and stuck his hand into it and pulled out a fistful of tiles.

''Let me see. What do I have here?'' he said, gazing at the tiles in the palm of his hand. ''What do you know? I think I can use all seven. It's two words, really. But that's in the spirit of Babble, isn't it?'' He leaned over the board and began to lay out his tiles horizontally facing her.

She peered at the first three letters. ''MAR,'' she read aloud.

''Wait till I finish,'' he said. He placed the four remaining tiles on the line.

''MAR RYME,'' she said. ''What is that—bad poetry? That's not how you spell *rhyme,* you know.''

''Kit, don't do this to me,'' he said, his gaze more serious than ever. His face had taken on a distinct pallor. He held out the bag of tiles for her to take.

"Okay, okay. I won't challenge the word," she said, reaching for the bag. It didn't rattle. There was something in it, but apparently not tiles. "What's this?" She loosened the drawstring and felt inside the bag. Her hand closed over a square velvet box. The bag fell away from her hand. She looked at the box and then down at the letters again—MARRY ME. "Oh," she breathed, and felt the warm rush of blood up her neck to her face. Her gaze locked with Ryan's.

"Aren't you going to open it?" he asked.

She couldn't look anywhere but at him. "Do you mean it, really mean it?"

He stood up, skirted the coffee table and knelt at her side. "I love you, which means I belong to you. Isn't that how it goes? Maybe you can live without me, but I can't make it another minute without you. Please marry me."

"Oh, Ryan." She fit her palm to his cheek. She could touch him now, whenever she wanted. She didn't have to hold back, or lecture herself anymore.

He took the small box from her and pulled a blazing solitaire from its velvet bed. She had to surrender the sweet feel of his rough beard on her hand so he could slide the ring on her finger.

"Oh, Ryan," she whispered again.

"If you don't say something other than 'Oh, Ryan,' you're going to send me around the bend."

She laughed and couldn't get any words out at all.

"I mean it, Kit. I have to know. So does Mary, so she can start planning the wedding. And, I suppose the manager of Shreve's would also like to know if it was worth it for him to open his store at five this morning for one man who was so desperately in love he couldn't wait till ten."

"I love you, too," she said, and threw herself into his arms. He mustn't have been balanced well on his knees, because he tipped over, and they both went down onto the floor.

He rolled over and trapped her beneath his body. "Now this is more like it."

"Yes, it is," she said, winding her arms around his neck and tugging his head toward hers.

He brought his lips within a breath of hers. "You haven't answered me yet."

She lifted her head to kiss him and he pulled back, his mouth a tantalizing inch away from hers.

"My answer, first," he said.

"Yes, yes, a thousand times, yes," she said.

"One 'yes' is all I need, thank you." And he kissed her.

*   *   *   *   *

MILLS & BOON®

*M*akes
any time
special

Enjoy a romantic novel from
Mills & Boon®

Presents...™   *Enchanted*™   TEMPTATION.

Historical Romance™   ⊸⋀MEDICAL
ROMANCE™

MILLS & BOON®

Enchanted™

THE SHEIKH'S REWARD by Lucy Gordon

Frances wanted an interview with Sheikh Ali Ben Saleem, and he agreed—on condition she accompany him to his kingdom. Once there, however, Frances found herself imprisoned by his concubines! What was more…Ali was insisting on marriage…

BRIDE ON LOAN by Leigh Michaels

Caleb Tanner needs a decoy to save him from the many women scheming to get him to the altar! Sabrina isn't thrilled about moving in with Caleb. He's too attractive for his own good. He's also her agency's biggest client so she has no choice but to play the bride-to-be.

HONEYMOON HITCH by Renee Roszel

Jake has made it clear that he wants children from his marriage of convenience with Susan. Yet, while Susan yearns for Jake's love without having even experienced a kiss from him, the most daunting thing on the horizon isn't their wedding day…but their wedding night!

A WIFE AT KIMBARA by Margaret Way

Brod Kinross suspects Rebecca of being a gold-digger, after his father's money. In fact it's not the money that Rebecca wants—or Brod's father—it's love and marriage to Brod himself…

Available from 5th May 2000